Irresistible Silver Fox Billionaire

Gwynne Hart

Contents

Introduction

My sister's billionaire ex and I failed Rule #1.
Fake fiancés should be just that—*Fake*

The ballroom falls silent as Carter Wright, broad-shouldered and impeccably dressed, enters. When his intense blue eyes lock with mine across the room, a jolt of heat electrifies me.

He's mistaken me for my sister... and I don't correct him. Even when he asks me to pretend to be his fiancée.

Furious upon discovering my deception, he continues the charade to secure his inheritance.

We play up this fiction with fervor, capturing the attention of the tabloids. Selling the sizzle is surprisingly easy.

Our heads know this is strictly business but our bodies don't. Fiction is now reality.

But a new threat is emerging.

Someone is scheming to destroy my newfound happiness and sabotage my shot at love.

Chapter One

Megan

I stride confidently through the opulent lobby of the Vivante Grand Hotel. The marble floors gleam under my heels from the chandeliers that cast a golden glow over the large space. There's a soft hum of conversation in the air and the distant sound of clinking glasses from the bar, giving the area a lively ambiance.

I've been to countless luxury hotels in my career, but the Vivante Grand is more extravagant than most. This place screams exclusivity, drawing in the Los Angeles elite by its grandeur. Even though this isn't my first time in such establishments, it's my first time here, and my body is buzzing with excitement and nerves.

Glancing at my watch, I realize the event I'm attending is already underway. The planning for a high-profile wedding contract is underway, and even though I usually send someone else to fully check out venues, this one is too important to delegate to one of my associates. The hotel's event manager invited me to an elite event happening at the hotel today so I can get an idea of their splendid production capabilities before the wedding.

Heading for the elevators, a deep voice grabs my attention. "Melissa?"

I turn, a bit puzzled. The man attached to the voice is tall, dressed in a sharp suit, with salt and pepper hair that gives him a distinguished look. His intense blue eyes seem to recognize me, but... I'm not Melissa.

It clicks. He thinks I'm my older sister. I'm about to correct him when he says, "Melissa Medina, it's been years! You haven't changed a bit." He approaches, his arms open wide in greeting.

On a whim, maybe because he's ridiculously handsome, or maybe because I'm curious, I decide to play along. "Good evening," I say with a smile, stepping into his embrace.

When he pulls back, there's clear admiration in his gaze. "You're even more stunning than I remember."

I can't help the blush that creeps up my cheeks. "Thank you," I say, trying to play the part of Melissa while my mind races. "And you are?"

He looks genuinely surprised. "You don't remember? I'm Carter. Carter Wright."

My heart skips a beat. Carter Wright. Billionaire. Owner of this hotel. Once, my teenage crush.

He chuckles softly. "Seems I left quite an impression back in college."

Oh, what a mess I've gotten myself into. "Carter! My mind was elsewhere." I lie, trying to keep up the facade. "It's just been so long."

His smile is genuine, but there's an arrogance to the way he holds himself. Even so, that gleaming smile and his angular cheekbones have a way of effortlessly luring me in.

"Yes, well, the last time I saw you, you were applying for a graduate program. Microbiology, was it? And your sister, what was her name—Maggie?"

"Megan," I reply. "M—her name is Megan."

"Megan...right? You always were the academic, Melissa. How is that underachiever of a little sister doing now?"

I bristle, unable to help myself, but the way he looks at me, all sultry blue eyes and a confident smirk, has me melting. If he thinks I'm Melissa, who am I to correct him? Even though there's eight years between us, Melissa and I are now often mistaken for twins.

"She's doing fine," I say cagily.

"Good to hear. Well, I can't talk right now. Can we catch up sometime? Call my office, ask for Margot."

"Er...sure. I'd love to."

I watch Carter walk away, his confident gait a stark contrast to the tumultuous feelings he's stirred deep inside me. He's undeniably attractive—not just his looks, but the aura of power and wealth surrounding him. And yet, despite all his worldliness, he couldn't tell the difference between me and Melissa. The realization stings my pride.

For a fleeting moment, guilt gnaws at my conscience for leading him on, but then a defiant thought strikes me: *If he can't distinguish me from my sister, why am I the one wrestling with remorse? He's the one who made the mistake, not me.*

Shaking off the conflicting emotions, I continue my journey to the event venue. The event has already kicked off, and the grand ballroom entrance is draped with luxurious gold and ivory fabrics. The soft, melodic tunes of a live quartet float through the air, and the sparkling lights make everything seem magical. I've attended high end party events before, of course, but nothing this extravagant.

It hits me then that I'm underdressed. Not horribly so, but enough to stand out. My simple black dress and modest heels are a far cry from the glamorous outfits most women are wearing.

Jewel-encrusted dresses, sky-high stilettos, and professionally done makeup—I suddenly feel like I've walked onto a movie set.

Determined not to be deterred, I take a deep breath and stride in. I'm here to observe and assess, and my attire isn't going to hinder my ability to do my job. Nevertheless, as I navigate the crowd, I can't shake off the feeling of being out of my element. Conversations around me buzz with mentions of exotic vacations, high-stake business deals, and the latest fashion trends from Paris and Milan. It's a bit overwhelming.

A server glides by, offering champagne. I take a glass, hoping it'll ease my nerves. As I take a sip, I overhear a group of women discussing the Vivante's owner—Carter Wright.

"He's such a mystery," one of them says, twirling a strand of her pearl necklace. "I've heard he's seeing someone."

"Impossible," another says with a smirk. "Carter Wright is married to his work."

Their chatter gives me pause. The man they're discussing—the billionaire who just mistook me for my sister—could be right here, somewhere in this room.

Before I can contemplate this further, a familiar face comes into view. It's Tim Donnelly, an events coordinator here at the hotel. I have worked with him on a few wedding events at other Vivante Group hotels in the past.

"Megan?" he questions, his eyebrows shooting up in surprise. "I wasn't expecting to see you here."

"We're planning a wedding here soon. Final planning," I say, trying to play it cool.

He gives a knowing smirk. "Or perhaps getting to know the owner a bit better? I saw you in the hall earlier."

I start to roll my eyes, but he continues. "I have news to share. I've just been promoted to events lead at this hotel."

"Oh, I didn't know. Congratulations. Has Jacinta left? I was just speaking to her earlier today."

"No, Jacinta's also been promoted to Event Director. She will be overseeing the management of events across the entire Vivante Group. It was just announced this afternoon."

Before I can respond, the quartet starts playing a slow waltz, drawing couples to the dance floor.

Tim extends a hand, a playful challenge in his eyes. "Care to dance?"

Tim's outstretched hand hovers expectantly in the space between us, and his smirk seems more a challenge than a friendly invitation. I've never been particularly fond of him. There's something in the way he interacts, a kind of feigned niceness, that I find grating; but if I want to maintain good relationships with this hotel group, brushing off the new hotel events manager is not the right move.

I sigh inwardly, plastering my best professional smile onto my face. "Of course."

As the waltz begins and Tim takes the lead, the closeness feels more confining than intimate. His chatter only makes the sensation worse. "You know, I heard the Morrison deal is falling through," he starts, trying to sound knowledgeable. "If you wanted to expand your business, join a proper company, now would be the time."

The information flows past me, largely irrelevant to my interests. I've told him time and time again that I'm happy where I am, and I enjoy the freedom of being self-employed.

All the while, my mind keeps drifting back to Carter. That striking figure from earlier, with his intense gaze and confident demeanor—it's a far cry from the college boy I once knew. Back then, I harbored a little crush on him, though he hardly noticed I existed. That was years ago, back when I was Melissa's shadow, the younger Medina girl who was always in the background. I'm surprised he even remembered Melissa had a sister despite not remembering my name.

A sudden tug brings me back to the present. Tim is trying to execute a fancy turn, pulling me closer in the process. I stifle my discomfort, taking a step back to regain my balance.

"Tim, maybe we should keep it simple," I suggest, not hiding the irritation in my voice.

He chuckles, brushing off my comment. "Always the reserved one, weren't you? You know, Megan, sometimes you need to take risks to get noticed."

His implication isn't lost on me. It's not the dance he's talking about, but my place in this world—among the elite, the powerful. All I can think about is the enigmatic Carter Wright. How would he react if he knew the truth? That the woman he thinks is Melissa Medina is actually her younger sister? The one he called an underachiever.

The music comes to an end, and I use the opportunity to extricate myself from Tim's grasp. "Thank you for the dance," I say, eager to distance myself from him and his gossip.

He nods, looking somewhat smug, but doesn't press further. I move through the crowd, assessing my next move. The night is still young, and I'm not ready to leave just yet.

As I walk away, I cast a quick glance over my shoulder. Sure enough, Tim stands there, a deep scowl marking his usually composed face. Some part of me feels a rush of satisfaction; another is wary of the brewing animosity and the consequences that could arise because of it.

Seeking escape, I make my way to the bar, signaling the bartender for a glass of white wine. As I wait, I overhear a group of event organizers discussing the arrangements for the evening. I recognize one of them, Sienna, from a wedding I had coordinated a couple of months ago at a different venue. She spots me and waves me over.

"Hey! Megan, right? The wedding planner?" She asks, her face lighting up with recognition.

"That's me," I reply with a small smile, appreciating a familiar face in this sea of strangers.

The organizers make small talk, discussing the latest trends in the event planning world. I chime in occasionally, sharing my own experiences and insights. It feels good to be in my element.

As the conversation progresses, I take a chance and inquire about Carter. "So, where is the man of the hour? I'd expect him to attend his own party."

Sienna chuckles. "You're new to Vivante Grand events, aren't you? Carter Wright hardly ever attends his own parties. The man owns a dozen hotels just in California, not to mention his international ventures. He doesn't really mingle with, well, the underlings."

A pang of disappointment hits me. I had hoped to get a chance to speak to him again, or at least see his face again. From the sounds of it, that seems unlikely tonight.

Still, the evening isn't a total loss. I'm confident the upcoming wedding will be spectacular. The networking has been productive, and I've collected a handful of business cards and swapped contacts with potential clients and collaborators.

Hours pass and the party is in full swing. The chatter grows louder, the music more vibrant, and the lights dimmer. Then, just as I'm about to call it a night, a hush falls over the room.

Carter Wright makes his entrance.

The crowd senses his presence and it electrifies the atmosphere. Conversations halt, glasses pause mid-air, and all eyes turn to him. Dressed in a sharp black tuxedo, his muscular frame exudes power and charisma that's difficult to ignore.

He doesn't linger, though. He makes his way to a private area, cordoned off from the main ballroom. Before he disappears, our eyes lock for a brief, charged moment. There's a flicker of recognition, but it's quickly replaced by the same impassive mask he had donned earlier.

Sienna notices my distraction and teases, "Caught your eye, did he?"

Blushing, I wave her off, trying to play it cool. "Just surprised he showed up, that's all.

Inside, my heart is thumping so loudly I can hear it in my ears.

"Busy day tomorrow, Sienna. Good night."

I leave the ballroom flabbergasted by the storm of conflicting emotions inside me. *What is happening to me?*

Chapter Two

Carter

Waking up in my penthouse bedroom, I feel a bone-deep exhaustion from last night's events. I was only at the party briefly. Seeing Melissa Medina after all these years has left me strangely unsettled. I never expected I could be carrying lingering feelings for her since our split back in college.

My phone vibrates with an incoming message, shaking me from my thoughts. I reach over, expecting some business-related update. Instead, it's a text from my brother, Colton.

Dad's in the hospital. It's bad. Get here ASAP.

Anger and panic compete for control as I grapple with the sudden urgency of his summons. If the old man can't text me himself on his old Blackberry, it must be bad. He knows I'd come regardless of our strained relationship. Fiercely controlling, he would never ask Colton to contact me. Not to mention, the last I knew, Colton was off traveling on business somewhere. How did he get notified of our dad's illness and get to the hospital before me?

I text my driver to meet me immediately. Taking a deep breath, I jump out of bed, quickly dressing in jeans and a simple shirt, not caring for the usual precision I give my attire.

The ride to the hospital is a blur, the skyscrapers and traffic melding into one long streak of gray. Each passing minute amplifies the weight in my chest. By the time I reach the hospital doors, my hands are shaking.

The hospital corridors seem to stretch endlessly, the smell of disinfectant and the hushed murmurs of the staff echoing around me. Following the directions I was given at the reception desk, I finally reach my father's room.

There he is, a once robust man now looking frail and pale, surrounded by beeping machines and a tangle of wires. He's conscious, eyes glazed but still sharp, watching me as I approach.

"Liver failure," he rasps without preamble, a shadow of his usual authoritative tone. "Years of drinking and my own foolishness."

I swallow hard, words sticking in my throat. Despite our differences, the sight of him like this is jarring. "Why didn't you tell me, Dad?"

He smirks, the gesture more painful than sardonic. "Thought you were too busy with your empire to notice. I didn't want to distract you."

Guilt and irritation strike me. Maybe I was immersed in my work, but he knows that's not the whole truth. "You should've called," I retort, voice thick with anger and worry.

He gives a weak chuckle. "Always the stubborn one. Just like your mother."

The mention of her brings an old, familiar ache. We sit in silence for a while, each lost in our own memories, time is a luxury we don't have.

"Colton said it was time to call you."

I stare at my father, trying to process what he just said. Colton had convinced him to reach out? The same brother I haven't spoken to in years? Who left all of us years ago when our mom was sick? To supposedly find his way in the world.

"You didn't call me but you called Colton? Why is he here?"

Dad coughs, his frail body shuddering momentarily. "Yes. He's changed. He's been... around for a while. Helping with the doctors, the treatments."

That revelation stings. "So you called him, but not me."

He looks at me, defiance in his eyes. "You know how Colton feels about you. The two of you never got along."

Anger surges within me. "You should've called me."

"Son, you could've called me."

The heaviness in the room intensifies, years of misunderstandings and disagreements pressing down on us. There is a reason we haven't spoken much since I took over the business. First, he pressures me into following the path he wants for me. Then, he wouldn't let go of the reins, and still will not let go. The years of growing up under his controlling behavior has left me disillusioned with the concept of having a close, loving family. I continue the business for my own sake, not *his*.

As I'm thinking about this, Dad drops another bombshell.

"I'm leaving everything to you," he says, his gaze unwavering.

That is a surprise. "Everything?"

He nods. "You've outdone yourself. Created an empire, elevated our family and the Vivante name. You're my most successful son."

It's a hollow victory. I never craved the empire or the wealth as much as I yearned for moments of genuine pride from him. Finally, I've earned it.

But I know him. There's always a catch. I wait.

Sure enough, he adds, "There's one condition."

A sense of dread settles in. "What is it?"

11

His voice is firm. "I want you to settle down. Find someone and start a family. Don't end up surrounded only by the cold comforts of concrete and steel."

I laugh, but there's no joy in it. "My inheritance is tied to my marital status? This is ludicrous!"

His eyes harden. "It's my final wish, Carter. You want the Vivante empire? This is the price."

I've always sensed the competition he's fostered between Colton and me. Now, even in this fragile state, he's setting the stage for yet another challenge.

"Why?" I ask, frustration evident. "Why can't you just let me be?"

He frowns, deep lines of regret etched on his face. "I know the ravages of loneliness, Carter. After your mother's passing, it's been a slow, relentless pain. I don't wish that on you."

I'm a mess of emotions. Resentment, grief, and anger are all swirling inside me.

"You have until I pass," he whispers, his eyes a mix of hope and defiance.

The ultimatum hangs heavy, altering my path in ways I can't even fathom. Sitting beside my sick father, I'm flooded with emotions. Above all, I feel cornered.

"If you don't marry by the time I'm gone, everything goes to Colton," he says, his voice feeble but resolute.

"Colton?" I exclaim, my voice raising in disbelief. "You mean the same Colton who partied through university and around the world?"

Dad's eyes dart to the framed photos on the bedside table. New pictures of Colton, his wife, and their two kids. A perfect little family. "He has a family now, Carter. A wife, children. He's settled. Turns out he's a very good manager and I have faith that he can handle Vivante Group business. If anything, he needs the money. You don't."

I can't contain my frustration any longer. "So just because he settled for an average life, had kids, and did the whole suburban dream, he gets everything? Despite everything I've done for the family business? For our name?"

Dad's expression is a mix of sadness and determination. "It's not about the business, Carter. It's about legacy. A family. I don't want our name, our lineage, to end with you."

"That's what this is about?" I snap. "Legacy? I've given my life to expand the business, worked tirelessly to make Vivante Group and the Wright family name synonymous with success. And you're saying that none of that matters because I haven't settled down and popped out a few kids?"

His eyes shimmer with unshed tears. "I've always tried to steer you both toward what I believed was best. You listened to me, he rebelled and found his own way, the difficult way. You are my most successful son, but I won't apologize for wanting you to find happiness outside of boardrooms and business deals."

The air thickens with tension. Anger burns within me. "Why, Dad? Why must you always pit Colton and I against each other?"

Before he can reply, the door bursts open. A nurse, her face a mix of concern and irritation, stands there. "Sir, I need to ask you to lower your voice. This is a hospital, and your father needs his rest."

I glance back at Dad, who looks more exhausted than ever. Swallowing my anger, I mutter a quick apology and make my way out the door, my steps heavy.

The world outside the hospital seems too bright, too noisy. I text my driver, lost in thought. Dad's words replay in my mind, stirring nausea in my stomach. The ultimatum feels like a chain around my neck, choking me with its weight.

Before I know it, we're back at the Vivante Grand. I step out, steeling myself for the board meeting ahead. The towering skyscraper, with its gleaming glass facade and the proud Vivante logo, stands as a testament to all my hard work. Yet today, it feels more like a gilded cage.

Inside, employees greet me with nods and smiles, but I barely register them. I head straight to the elevator, pressing the button for the executive floor, where the board awaits my briefing.

As the doors close and the elevator begins its ascent, all I can think of are my father's demands and the impossible choice he's forced upon me.

After the board meeting, which felt way too long despite its brevity, I head for the elevators. My mind is burdened by the meeting's details, my father's condition, and his confounding ultimatum.

Rounding a corner, I catch a flash of a familiar brunette. It's her—Melissa. She's animatedly discussing something with a group of people, her expressive hands moving as she speaks. A portfolio of sorts rests under her arm.

I slow my pace, curious. "...so the floral arrangements will be here and the main seating here... " Her voice carries a note of authority, surprising me. I thought she was into microbiology.

It's only when someone in the group mentions a *high-profile wedding* and *extensive coverage* that it clicks. She's a wedding planner? That's a far cry from microbiology. She must have changed career paths somewhere along the way.

Before I can contemplate further or even approach her, she's swiftly moving toward the elevators, leaving her entourage behind. Intrigued, I decide to follow at a distance. If she's organizing a major wedding at the Vivante Grand, chances are our paths are bound to cross more often. Maybe, just maybe, there's an opportunity here to get to know her again, properly.

I overhear one of her associates as I pass by, "Miss Medina certainly knows how to handle these elite events."

Reaching the elevators just as the doors slide shut with her inside, I press the call button and wait. An idea starts to form, a way to approach her without making it seem too forward. Business always provides a good pretense for introductions, or, in this case, re-introductions.

While descending, I pull out my phone and quickly send a message to my secretary, Margot, asking her to find out more about this wedding Miss Medina is planning. A little background could provide the necessary icebreaker.

The doors open to the grand lobby, and I spot her standing near the exit. She's taking a moment, looking at the grandeur of the hotel's interior. There's an excited glint in her roving eyes, evaluating options and possibilities.

Swallowing the hesitation, I approach her. "Melissa? Or do you prefer Miss Medina?" I greet, a friendly smile playing on my lips.

She turns, surprise evident in her eyes. "Carter Wright," she says, an unreadable expression settling on her face. "Either will do." There's a tone of mischief, a playful challenge. The game is on.

That's odd. I recall Melissa being more serious, less playful but more outspoken. "Of course," I respond, though something doesn't feel quite right. "Last I heard, you were studying microbiology? Biotech? How'd you shift from that to wedding planning?"

She shrugs gracefully, her eyes sparkling with mischief. "People change. Interests evolve. Besides, who wouldn't want to plan the happiest day of people's lives?"

Our conversation drifts to the upcoming high-profile wedding. "Whitney Barker, the renowned violinist," she offers. "She's marrying Landon Davis. It's still in the early stages, but I'm hopeful."

"Whitney and Landon? That's big," I comment, impressed despite myself. "Well, the Vivante Grand is the best venue in town. I'm sure the wedding will be remarkable."

There's an unmistakable tension in her stance, a subtle nervousness I don't remember Melissa ever having. "I hope so. It's a golden opportunity."

Our exchange feels both familiar and new. The surroundings, the context, it's all lavish and high-end. Even so, there's an underlying layer, a dance of memories and new impressions. She seems both like the Melissa I remember and a complete stranger.

As our chat winds down, she checks her watch. "I should head out. I'm meeting Whitney and Landon soon."

"Good luck," I say.

"Thanks," she responds as she turns to walk away.

I watch her as she walks toward the café off the lobby. I feel captivated by the enigma, she's not entirely the Melissa I remember, but that only piques my interest further.

Chapter Three

Megan

The upscale café attached to the Vivante Grand hums with chatter, its decadent atmosphere adding to the significance of the meeting. Whitney Barker, an elegant vision in silk, and her fiancé, Landon Davis, sit across from me. Every detail about them screams of their wealth.

"So, Miss Medina," Whitney begins, her voice soft yet assertive, "tell us why you think you're the right fit to plan our wedding?"

Confidence bubbles within me. "I've coordinated many successful events at various Vivante hotels. My attention to detail, passion for creating magical moments, and intricate knowledge of the venue makes me an ideal choice."

"A wedding like ours is more personal than other events. More *esteemed*. You must know from planning your own wedding how personal and perfect you want it to be."

My heart stumbles a bit. "I'm not married."

"Don't you think a wedding planner should have firsthand experience? How can you understand the intricacies of love and marriage without having been through it yourself?"

I fight to keep my composure. "Love and marriage are beautiful, but you don't need to be married to appreciate that and understand their importance. My work speaks for itself."

Landon chimes in, trying to ease the tension. "Whitney, we have received many recommendations for Miss Medina. Let's give her a chance."

Whitney persists, "I just think a wedding planner should be married. Or at least engaged. It adds authenticity, don't you think?"

Desperation makes my mind whirl. "Actually," I blurt out, "I am engaged."

Whitney's eyes widen in genuine surprise, while Landon raises an eyebrow. "Oh? Congratulations! That's wonderful news," Whitney says, the hint of skepticism still present in her voice. "Where's your ring?"

"It's... being resized. I lost some weight recently, and it kept slipping off."

"I see. Well, that changes things slightly. It's just that a wedding is so personal, and I'd like to work with someone who truly understands its importance."

My lie weighs heavily on my chest, but I force a smile. "I completely understand, Miss Barker. I assure you, I am fully prepared to make your day as special as you've ever dreamed."

Landon, convinced, offers his hand. "Looking forward to working with you, Miss Medina."

I shake his hand, relief flooding me. Whitney's scrutinizing gaze hasn't yet disappeared. "I hope we've made the right choice," she says quietly, almost to herself.

The meeting concludes shortly after, and as I leave, the reality of my impulsive lie begins to truly sink in. What have I gotten myself into?

Walking out of the café and back into the lobby of the Vivante Grand, I exhale deeply, trying to shake off the unease from my meeting with Whitney and Landon. I mentally chastise myself for the lie I just spun, unsure of how I'll navigate the complications it might bring.

"Miss Medina."

Startled, I look up and find myself face-to-face with Carter Wright, again. His piercing gaze is intense, and a shiver runs down my spine. It's bizarre that after all these years, he still remembers "me" as "Melissa."

"Oh, Mr. Wright," I say, attempting nonchalance. "Fancy seeing you here."

A smirk dances on his lips. "Considering I own the place, it shouldn't be that surprising."

I roll my eyes, even though my heart flutters. "Fair point."

He takes a step closer, his voice a low whisper. "I've been looking for you, actually."

"Have you?" I raise an eyebrow, curious. "Why's that?"

"I need your number," he states plainly. My surprise must be evident because he adds, "For business reasons, of course."

I tilt my head, suspicious. "What business could you possibly have with a wedding planner?"

Carter hesitates momentarily, glancing around the bustling lobby. "Can we discuss this somewhere more private?"

The request catches me off guard, but I nod in agreement. He leads me to a secluded meeting room, and once inside, he closes the door, adding to the sense of intimacy. The room feels too small, the air charged with a tension I can't quite place.

"Alright," I start, leaning against the polished oak table. "What's this all about?"

He takes a deep breath, as if gathering himself. "I need to get married. Quickly."

19

I blink, thrown by the abruptness of the confession. "Well, I'm a wedding planner, not a matchmaker, Mr. Wright."

"That's not what I meant." He steps closer, his gaze unwavering. "I need you to pose as my fiancée."

A stunned laugh escapes me. "You can't be serious."

He's deadly serious. "I am."

"Why on earth would you ask me?"

"Because," he begins, pinching the bridge of his nose in evident frustration, "circumstances have arisen. My father's health, the will, the stipulations... It's complicated."

I frown. "Your father's unwell?"

"Very."

"Oh. I'm sorry to hear that."

He shrugs. "Don't be. You never met him, and I'd rather not discuss it anyway. So, about our deal?"

I study him, seeing the genuine desperation in his eyes. I can tell it's about more than just his father. "Even if I were to consider it, what's in it for me?"

Carter straightens, regaining some of his usual composure. "A substantial amount of money, for one. Of course, the prestige of having the Vivante Grand or any of our other hotels as a guaranteed venue for all your future events. Think about it, Melissa. The publicity alone would skyrocket your business."

I'm torn between incredulity and temptation. The benefits are undeniable, but the risk... I look at Carter, the billionaire businessman, wondering what has brought him to this point of desperation. For a fleeting moment, I consider it.

There's also the small issue of the fact I've just told my two highest profile clients I'm engaged. The coincidental timing seems too good to be true; and that alone is enough to make me wary.

"Give me time to think about it," I finally say, my voice steady.

He nods, relief evident in his gaze. "Sure."

As I leave the meeting room, the situation begins to truly sink in. Two lies within 24 hours, and my life has suddenly become extremely complicated.

Lost in thought, I barely notice the thrum of the city as I make my way to the parking lot. Carter's proposal replays in my mind on a loop. The benefits are unmistakably attractive—financial stability, a surge in my business's reputation, and an alliance with one of Los Angeles's most influential men. The very convenience of the offer raises red flags. Why me? Of all people?

Pulling my phone from my bag, I stare at the screen for a long moment. A part of me wants to text him and agree, but prudence wins. I need to understand all the strings attached. Every deal, especially one this tempting, has its caveats.

I'm also aware my teenage crush is back in action. Carter's chiseled face is popping into my head all too frequently. When I enter the Vivante Grand, I yearn for a glimpse of him, in his bespoke suits that hug his sexy, elegant physique so perfectly.

Okay, Megan, let's be logical, I say to myself. With a deep breath, I type out a message, suggesting we meet to iron out the specifics of this... arrangement. I pick a local café I visit often, one with quiet corners perfect for private conversations.

Almost immediately, a notification pops up, indicating Carter has replied. I quickly open the message, my heart beating a tad faster.

That café might be your style, but it's a bit pedestrian for my taste, he writes with a teasing arrogance. *How about Cielo Bleu? Seven o'clock tomorrow night?*

My jaw drops slightly. Cielo Bleu is one of the most luxurious dining spots in the city. The kind of place that's perpetually booked and requires a considerable waiting list. Not to mention, one dinner there could likely drain a month's rent from my account.

Reeling in my initial shock, I shoot back a response, trying to infuse my text with as much nonchalance as possible. *Sure, if you're buying.*

Within seconds, his response arrives: *Naturally. See you then Melissa.*

The use of the alias, the identity he believes me to be, leaves a bitter taste in my mouth. I shake my head, dismissing the building guilt. If he can't recognize the difference between Melissa and I, then maybe he deserves a little deception.

Pushing the pending confrontation to the back of my mind, I focus on our upcoming meeting. It's essential to lay down clear boundaries and understand his expectations. More importantly, I need to gauge the risks involved. Getting entangled with a man like Carter Wright isn't child's play, and I refuse to be a pawn in a larger game that could end in devastating consequences.

Sliding into my car, I start the engine, the gentle purr oddly comforting. One thing's for sure; my life has taken a turn I hadn't anticipated. As I drive off, the city lights blur, reflecting my muddled thoughts.

Is this arrangement a golden opportunity? Or am I teetering on the edge of a precipice, dangerously close to tumbling into chaos? Only time will tell.

The L.A. skyline fades into a smear of golden and blue hues as I drive through familiar streets, passing the familiar storefronts of my neighborhood. Everything blurs together, my thoughts consuming me and drowning out the honks and chatter of the early evening traffic.

Pulling up to my building—a relic from the early nineteen-hundreds—I park my car and head inside. The entrance is dull with fluorescent lights buzzing overhead, starkly contrasting with the chandeliers and warm ambient lighting of the Vivante Grand Hotel. The musty smell of old wood and fading paint greets me, a scent that usually brings comfort. But now, in the wake of today's events, it only amplifies the stark difference between Carter's world and mine.

I wait for the aged elevator, and a pang of envy twists in my stomach. Here I am, living paycheck to paycheck, while a man like Carter has the power to change my life with a single, albeit bizarre, proposition. The elevator groans to life, its slow ascent emphasizing the building's age. I shake off the negative thoughts, reminding myself of the hard work I've put into my business and the passion I have for my job.

Reaching my apartment, I collapse onto my worn-out, second-hand sofa and let out a long sigh. I'm overwhelmed by everything—the roller coaster of the day, the looming lies, the storm of emotions that swirl inside me. *Stay logical. Don't think about Mr. Sexy.*

I groan to myself. I should come clean. The thought loops in my mind. But how? Carter Wright is infatuated with a memory—a vivacious, confident Melissa, who sharply contrasts the Megan that I am. The Megan who used to tag along, often eclipsed by her older sister's charisma. Revealing the truth now could shatter his perception of me and potentially jeopardize the advantageous position I've found myself in thanks to his error.

I'm tempted to text him, to unveil the truth and brace for the fallout. Yet fear holds me back—the fear of rejection, of being labeled a fraud, of losing the chance to elevate my business to levels I've dreamed of my whole life. The knowledge of these daunting choices bears down on me, the potential outcomes piling up, each a pressing layer threatening to overwhelm my resolve.

Chapter Four

Carter

The opulence of Cielo Bleu is undeniable, even to someone like me who has frequented many of the world's most luxurious places. Crystal chandeliers hang from the high ceilings, and the soft glow of ambient light illuminates the decadent interior. I glance at my watch for the umpteenth time, noting with a jolt of annoyance that she's late.

The soft murmurs of other patrons and the clinking of fine china are interrupted when the door swings open. In walks Melissa. Her slightly breathless appearance makes it clear she's rushed to get here. Her curves are captivating, reminding me of times past, but I can't help my immediate reaction. "You're late," I observe coolly.

"Maybe if you didn't choose the most pompous, inaccessible place in the city, I'd be on time," she snaps back.

Before the tension can escalate, a petite waitress with a perfectly coiled bun steps up to our table, offering us a menu and a polite smile that seems to ease the previous friction. I don't miss the relief in Melissa's eyes.

"Wine?" I ask, not really seeking her opinion.

She nods, "Sure."

"A bottle of the Pomerol, please," I tell the waitress, who nods and quickly walks away.

I lean forward, resting my elbows on the table, studying her. Memories of the intense heat between us in college intrude into my thoughts without warning, and I forcefully suppress them. "Here's the deal," I begin, taking a deep breath to lay out my terms. "We get engaged, formally and publicly. After a reasonable period—say a few months, we have a wedding. It needs to be convincing."

She raises an eyebrow, incredulity flickering in her eyes. "Go on," she prompts.

"You'll move into my penthouse. It's spacious, so you'll have your own wing. We maintain appearances in public, but behind closed doors, we don't even have to acknowledge each other if we don't want to. You'll have complete autonomy; run your business, meet your friends, whatever. Just... when we're out, when there are eyes on us, it has to look real. Can you do that?"

She takes a moment, her gaze drifting to a point beyond my shoulder as she considers the proposition. I can almost hear the gears turning in her head, weighing the pros and cons. It's a lot to ask of someone, but I'm desperate, and I have a hunch that she is too.

Finally, her eyes meet mine with a determined glint. "So, we play house, make it believable, and then what? After the wedding?"

I shrug, "An arrangement like this has terms. We can discuss the details later, but for now, are you in or out?"

She takes a deep breath, her shoulders rising and falling with the action. "Let's discuss the terms in detail. I'm leaning toward doing it."

I nod, trying to mask the relief that floods through me. The waitress returns, placing the bottle of wine between us—a symbol, perhaps, of the deal we're on the verge of sealing.

She's silent for a moment, processing my offer. Then she tilts her head, her soft curls bouncing with the motion. "Alright, if we're doing this, I have my own conditions."

I quirk an eyebrow, curious. "Go on."

Melissa takes a deep breath, clearly rehearsing her words in her head before speaking. "Firstly, there's my payment. I want the money in monthly installments, like a paycheck. Deposited straight into my bank—no cash, no checks."

I raise my eyebrows, impressed by her audacity. Not many people would have the guts to demand that up front. I respect her for it.

"Secondly," she says, "I want to use this engagement to secure some high-profile clients. Claire Beaujolais and her new fiancé, for instance. The exposure would be invaluable for my business."

I nod slowly, processing her demands. "That's fair. Anything else?"

She hesitates for a brief moment. "Once it's all said and done, we have a public falling out. Give it a few weeks to make it look natural. A heartbreaking split, and then a quiet divorce. We go our separate ways, and that's the end of it."

It's clear she's put a lot of thought into this. She's already mapped out our entire faux relationship. I have to admit, it's thorough and it's smart. "Agreed," I say, "Is that all?"

She glances down at her hands, then meets my gaze again. "I want to make it clear that while we'll be playing a couple, there won't be any... intimacy."

I chuckle, finding her directness refreshing. "Understood. Although, we might need to fake it some for the cameras."

Melissa's cheeks redden at that, but she nods. "Fine, but no actual intimacy."

We're both quiet for a moment, then I break the silence. "So, we have a deal?"

She hesitates, chewing her bottom lip, before nodding. "Yes, we have a deal."

I extend my hand across the table, expecting her to shake it. She doesn't. Instead, she gives me a pointed look, her green eyes sharp.

"You seem rather flippant about all this," she comments, her voice taking on a slightly colder tone.

I withdraw my hand, surprised by her change in demeanor. "Flippant?"

"Yes," she says, her voice steady. "This is a big deal for both of us, but you're treating it like it's some casual business transaction."

I frown, trying to gauge where this is coming from. "It is a business transaction."

Melissa shakes her head, clearly frustrated. "It's not just that. It's our lives, Carter. We're talking about pretending to be in love, getting married, and all you can do is talk about terms and conditions. Do you even care about how this might affect us?"

I'm stunned. I hadn't expected this level of emotion from her. "Of course I care," I say, trying to keep my voice calm. "This is the only way I can think of to get what I need."

She snorts, rolling her eyes. "Typical. You're only thinking of yourself."

Taking a deep breath, I steady myself. "Look, Melissa," I begin, aiming for a truce. "This isn't personal. It's strictly business."

Her eyebrows narrow sharply. "Do you even hear yourself? We're talking about marriage, Carter. You want me to wear a ring, pretend to be in love with you, move in together, and to you it's just another business deal?"

The defensive wall goes up instantly. "You are in on this agreement too, right? If you want something more emotional or genuine, then maybe this isn't the best choice for you."

She stands her ground, fiery determination in her eyes. "Just because I agreed to this doesn't mean you get to belittle me. I'm trying to say that being callous about this is how we're going to get found out."

Rubbing my temples, the stress of the conversation presses down. "Melissa, I'm not trying to belittle you. I'm laying out the facts. I offer something you want, and you offer something I need. That's business."

She's seething now. "But it's not typical business, and acting like it's just business is going to cause trouble; what if emotions get involved?"

I can't help but scoff. "Emotions? Like this annoyance I'm feeling?"

Her smirk is a bit wry. "That's what I'm talking about."

The tension is a thick force between us. Just when I think we'll continue in this standoff, she lets out a heavy sigh. "Listen," she starts, tone softer. "If this is going to work, we have to at least try to get along. We need to be believable."

I look at her, surprised by this mercurial shift. There's a steel in her eyes, a sort of determination that's surprisingly captivating. Not like the Melissa I remember. She's testing me.

"You're right," I concede, sipping my wine. "We need to cooperate for this arrangement to work. I'm willing if you are."

She gives a slow nod. "Fine. Let's make it a point to communicate. No more bickering. We're in this together."

There's a smirk on my lips. "Deal."

She offers her hand, and when I take it, a surprising charge races up my arm. The sensation throws me off; it's entirely unexpected. For a fleeting second, I wonder if our past attraction is still there, if I was genuinely close to her, but that's a dangerous road to go down.

She breaks the silence. "So, it's settled then?"

Meeting her gaze, I nod, "It's settled."

"Are we going to write up a contract?"

"And risk someone finding it by mistake? I don't think so."

Her lips twist into a delicate scowl. "Fair enough. Whatever this is, it promises to be one hell of a ride."

The two of us sit in a weighty silence. Each of us occasionally takes a sip from our glasses, letting the taste of the wine break the tension.

Every so often, I catch myself stealing glances in her direction. The Melissa I remember from college was confident, no doubt, but always in the center of some drama. This woman in front of me, she's different. She exudes a quiet strength, a fierce independence that I hadn't seen before. I find myself drawn to it, trying to reconcile the memories of a younger Melissa with the alluring woman before me.

To break the silence, I attempt some small talk. "So, how did you get into wedding planning?"

She smiles wryly, and there's a playfulness in her eyes. "I've always been good at organizing events, ever since school. Just never thought I'd turn it into a career. How about you? Did you always know you'd be a hotel mogul?"

I chuckle. "Well, no and yes, don't you remember? My father was insistent I join the family business. At the bottom, though. Didn't give me any other choice. I had to work my way up. Fought him all the way. After my father retired, I was the only one who could take over. Life is funny like that."

She nods, looking deep in thought. "It sure is."

There's a vulnerability to her now. It's as if all the walls she built have come crumbling down for a moment. It's endearing, and it draws me to her. I'm no longer seeing her as just a business arrangement but as Melissa, someone who's been through highs and lows and come out stronger, and I can't deny my attraction to her. It's time to leave before I blow this business deal to shreds.

Finishing my glass, I signal for the bill.

I notice her watching me, her gaze smoldering. Something's changed between us. There's an unspoken understanding, a simmering tension between us.

Looking up after I settle the bill, our eyes lock. I lean across the table and our lips meet. It's tentative at first, a brush of lips, but then it deepens. It's as if a dormant fire has been ignited.

Pulling back, our eyes meet. Both of us seem equally stunned.

"I shouldn't have done that," I say.

She shakes her head slightly, her cheeks flushed. "No need. It was... unexpected, but not unwelcome."

We sit there for a moment, processing what just transpired. It's a game changer, no doubt. What was initially just a business deal now has an added layer of complexity.

Instead of regret or hesitation, all I feel is an undeniable pull toward her, an attraction that seems to be growing by the second.

Clearing my throat, I manage to find my voice. "Well, this evening turned out to be more eventful than I expected."

She grins, the atmosphere suddenly lighter. "I'd have to agree."

We step out into the cool night air, the city's soft buzz enveloping us. It's a stark contrast to the intense warmth I felt moments ago. We begin to walk side by side, but she stops suddenly, causing me to turn toward her.

"I want to kiss you again," she whispers, her eyes reflecting the glow of the nearby streetlights.

I'm taken aback for a moment, but any surprise is quickly replaced by an intense longing. Without further words, our lips meet once more. It starts gently, explorative, our mouths tasting and testing each other. As seconds pass, the kiss deepens, becoming more urgent, more desperate.

Melissa's hands travel up my chest, pulling me closer, and I respond in kind. My hand finds its way into her hair, fingers curling around the soft strands, holding her against me. With my free hand, I brace myself on the brick wall of the nearby building, gently maneuvering her back up against it. The rough texture of the brick contrasts with the softness of her skin as our bodies press together.

Every touch, every sound, every breath becomes amplified, drowning out the noise of the surrounding city. I can feel the rapid beating of her heart against my chest, matching the excited rhythm of my own.

Finally, breathless and heated, we pull apart. Our foreheads rest against each other, our rapid breaths mingling in the small space between us.

She chuckles lightly, a sound that's both sultry and teasing. "If that's our practice round, I think our engagement will be quite the spectacle."

I laugh, the tension from moments ago now replaced with a lightness. "I'd have to agree. We make a convincing pair."

She grins, pushing herself off the wall, and smoothing out her dress. "Well, if we're going to do this, let's do it right. Full-on Hollywood romance."

I raise an eyebrow, intrigued. "I'm listening."

"We'll need a story. A first date, a moment we realized we were in love, and of course, the proposal. People eat up those stories. It'll make our engagement believable."

I nod, getting into the spirit of it. "Okay, let's say we met at a friend's wedding, where you were the planner. I was struck by your dedication and your passion for your work."

"I noticed you watching me from afar but was too focused on the job to approach you at the time. Our eyes met a couple of times... "

She's enjoying this. I grin and quip, "...and then we bumped into each other at the after-party, shared a dance, and the rest is history."

"It's perfect. It's romantic, it's believable, and it ties into our professions."

I grin, "Well then, fake fiancée, here's to our Hollywood love story."

Chapter Five

Megan

That dinner with Carter was the first of many. Once we had our plans outlined, it was much easier to be together, at least, to be seen in public.

Now it's time for another grand dinner, in another fancy restaurant, where I'll eat dishes I can't pronounce, and pretend that I want to be there.

Well, at least I'm getting used to it.

Pushing open the door to the upscale restaurant, I step into a world of glistening chandeliers, intimate candle-lit tables, and the soft hum of conversations. The fragrant aroma of gourmet dishes makes my stomach growl in anticipation. I've been to many fancy places at this point, but tonight feels different. There's an electric charge in the air, an awareness that every moment from here on out is a pivotal part of our staged romance.

As I scan the room, my eyes settle on Carter. He's seated at a table near the back, offering a prime view of the entire establishment. It's not the ambiance or the lavish surroundings that leave me breathless. It's him.

Carter looks every bit the dashing billionaire tonight. The tailored black suit he wears clings to his physique in all the right places, accentuating his broad shoulders and defined muscles. The crisp white shirt underneath contrasts starkly with his deep tan, and the silver cufflinks catching the light hint at his taste for luxury. What really captures my attention are his eyes. Those piercing blue eyes, which even from a distance, draw me into him.

Taking a deep breath, I make my way over, each step heightening my body's awareness of him. There's a magnetic pull, an attraction that I haven't felt in a long while, and I curse myself for it. This is just a business deal, I remind myself. Still, as I get closer, I can't help but appreciate the man before me.

He rises as I approach, a smile on his lips. "You look breathtaking," he murmurs, pulling out a chair for me.

"Thank you," I say, taking a seat and adjusting my dress. It's a deep red, hugging my curves and falling just above the knees. I'd chosen it specifically for the occasion, knowing how important it was to be noticeable tonight.

As we settle in, a sommelier appears by our side, recommending a bottle of one of the most expensive wines on the menu. I don't even blink as Carter agrees, signaling for him to pour us both a glass. It's intoxicating, the rich taste of the wine, the plush surroundings, and the knowledge that, at least for now, I belong in this world.

—ele—

The fine china clinks gently as the server places our appetizers in front of us. The fragrance of truffle oil and seared scallops fills the air. Everything looks delicious, but anticipation makes it hard to focus on the food.

"Why don't we just get it over with?" I suggest, trying to sound light-hearted, though my fingers tap anxiously on the table.

Carter glances at me, his eyes holding a flash of amusement. "Eager, are we?"

I give a half-laugh. "I just don't like dragging things out. Let's just... get on with it."

He takes a sip of his wine, eyes still locked on mine. "You'll make a fine actress, Melissa," he comments.

There's that name again. Every time he calls me *Melissa,* it's a stab to the gut, reminding me of the layers of deceit that have been woven into this arrangement.

"What if I'm not up to it?" I voice my concern, swirling the wine in my glass.

He raises an eyebrow. "You're doing a fine job pretending to be someone you're not."

I suppress a cringe. How apt his words are, but he has no idea of the extent. My mind drifts back to those high school days, a world where Melissa, well into college, was the star of the family. I was merely her shadow. Carter, being older than both of us, had always been drawn to Melissa. I was just the younger sister with a silent crush, hidden behind my books and dreams.

"You seem lost in thought. Nervous?" he asks, drawing me back to the present.

"Just... reflecting," I say. "We've come a long way from where we began, haven't we?"

He smirks. "Reminiscing about years gone by?"

I feel the heat rise to my cheeks. "Something like that, I suppose."

Carter chuckles. "You've grown into your own, Melissa. I must admit, you're not the young, wild girl I remember. You've become more... assertive. Stronger."

There's that name again—*Melissa*. My heart races. A part of me wants to yell out, correct him, tell him who I really am. Another, more selfish part enjoys the lifestyle and the attention too much to risk losing it all. Being with him, even under the guise of a lie, is an intoxicating thrill. Every glance, every touch, and every word exchanged teeters on the edge of truth and deception.

We continue our meal, the conversation flowing more freely as the wine loosens our inhibitions. The undercurrent of tension never truly dissipates. The knowledge that I'm on the brink of something monumental, mixed with the memory of my unrequited teenage love for him, makes everything so much more intense.

As the final dish is cleared away, Carter takes a deep breath, eyes scanning the restaurant briefly. There's an earnestness in his gaze as he turns back to me, a stark contrast to his earlier playful demeanor.

He reaches into his pocket, producing a small velvet box. I can feel the eyes of the diners nearby turning toward us, the gentle murmurs of conversation giving way to a thick, expectant silence.

"Melissa," he begins, and I feel another pang. "We've been through so much together, and though our journey might not have been typical, it's been... unique."

He opens the box to reveal a dazzling diamond ring. The stone is immense, its brilliance making my eyes widen. It's surrounded by smaller diamonds, glittering on a platinum band. The sheer opulence of it is staggering.

"I know this might seem sudden," he continues, his voice slightly shaky, but full of conviction. "and our path has been... unconventional; but, Melissa, will you marry me?"

I blink away the surprise, trying to keep my wits about me. This is all part of the show, but damn, he's good. The ring, the setting, his words—it's everything a girl could dream of, even if it's based on deception.

Taking a deep breath, I plaster on the most convincing smile I can muster, feeling a tear threaten to spill—a tear of happiness, confusion, or maybe just the weight of the moment, I'm not sure. "Yes, Carter. Yes, I will."

The restaurant breaks into applause, with a few gasps and excited whispers weaving through the atmosphere. I catch snippets of their conversations—*Did you see the size of that rock?*—but all I can focus on is the warmth of Carter's hand as he slides the ring onto my finger.

It's a perfect fit.

He leans over, pressing a soft kiss to my lips, pulling back to look into my eyes. "Thank you," he murmurs, so low that only I can hear.

"For what?" I ask, genuinely puzzled.

"For making this believable," he says with a hint of vulnerability.

I'm momentarily lost for words. Even though the proposal, the engagement, everything is a ruse, there's a raw honesty in this moment between us. An understanding that while we may be playing roles, the emotions aren't entirely feigned.

"We're a good match, even if it's fake," I admit, offering him a wry smile.

For a second, the lines between the facade and reality blur even further, and I wonder just where this twisted journey will lead us both.

The soft press of his lips against mine feels genuine, the heat speeding through me. There's no audience this time, just the two of us in this suspended moment. I can feel the rapid beating of his heart against my chest, and for a split second, I allow myself to get lost in the sensation.

As all fleeting moments do, it ends. He gently pulls away, eyes searching mine for a reaction. The silence between us is charged, neither of us quite sure what to say. It's a mutual agreement to leave the restaurant, to move away from the scene of our grand act.

The evening air is crisp as we walk to his sleek, black car. Without a word, he opens the door for me, the action reminding me once again of the disparity in our worlds. As he drives, the soft hum of the engine is the only sound between us. The bright lights of the city pass by in a blur, mirroring the emotions I'm grappling with on the inside.

Just when I think the ride will pass in silence, he breaks it, his voice a sharp contrast to the calm of the evening. "Remember, Melissa," he starts, and I'm reminded of the charade we're playing, "We have to start thinking about moving in together and planning the wedding." His tone is all business, with no glimpse of the man who just passionately kissed me mere minutes ago.

I let out a soft sigh, my emotions a jumbled mess. "I know, Carter," I say, trying to keep my voice steady, "Let's get started tomorrow."

He nods, and I notice his grip on the steering wheel tighten. The rest of the drive is silent, both of us lost in our thoughts.

Before I realize it, we're outside my apartment building. The familiar sight of it feels like a grounding force after the events of the evening.

He parks the car, turning off the ignition. "I'll see you tomorrow morning... I have nothing before 10. How's 9 a.m.?" he says, his voice softer, the rigid businessman facade slipping just a bit.

I nod, pausing before I open the door. "The sooner the better. Thank you, Carter. For everything."

He gives a brief nod, eyes unreadable. "Goodnight, Melissa."

Stepping out of the car, the weight of the evening presses down on me. I watch as he drives away, the taillights fading into the distance. As I head up to my apartment, I wonder what I've gotten myself into, and how on earth I'm going to navigate the complicated path ahead.

Chapter Six

Carter

The sun pours through the vast windows of my office, casting long shadows over the elegant hardwood floor. The city sprawls out beneath, a magnificent view that never fails to impress, but today my focus is elsewhere.

Melissa enters, slightly flustered, the soft hint of blush on her cheeks indicating her haste. Her hair is slightly tousled, and her breaths come in short, quick gasps. "I'm sorry," she begins, catching her breath, "this building... it's like a maze."

I suppress a small smile. "It can be a bit overwhelming the first few times," I admit.

She takes a seat across from my desk, smoothing out the wrinkles in her dress. We dive straight into the matter at hand, going over every detail of our upcoming sham of a wedding. "How long should we wait before getting married?" she asks, genuine curiosity in her voice.

I pause, collecting my thoughts. "My father isn't well, but he isn't on his last breath either. Maybe three or four months? Enough time for it to look real."

Melissa tilts her head thoughtfully, then asks, "Why not use this time to try to reconcile with him? Make things right?"

Her words strike a nerve, sharper than she probably intended. "That's not your business," I snap, more harshly than I mean to. Her eyes widen slightly, and I regret my outburst.

She takes a deep breath. "I'm sorry, I just thought—"

I cut her off, my voice tight with years of suppressed emotions. "Look, my relationship with my father is complicated. When I was a child, he was strict to the point of controlling. He never allowed me to do anything, watching my every move—and that only got worse once I reached adulthood. He has judged me for every little thing, my entire life. I don't even know if things can be fixed between us."

Melissa looks at me with a mixture of sympathy and understanding. "I'm sorry, Carter. I didn't know. I didn't mean to pry."

I run a hand through my hair, exhaling slowly. "It's private—my father and I. That's why I didn't tell you all of this back in the day. I shouldn't have snapped at you, but it really isn't your business." I meet her gaze, my eyes a little softer. "Let's just focus on our plan."

She nods in agreement, and we get back to ironing out the details, but a part of me lingers on the subject we've just broached. The wounds of the past are deep, and no charade, no matter how elaborate, can truly cover them up.

We continue discussing our faux wedding with a laser focus, trying to hash out every little detail to make it as believable as possible. It's strange—talking about wedding details as a business transaction, devoid of any real romantic intention.

"You should move in before the wedding but how soon?" I ponder aloud, looking to gauge her thoughts.

Melissa hesitates, "You're strangely determined to have me move in with you."

I scoff. "Yes, obviously. What married couple doesn't live together?"

I notice Melissa scowl, nose crinkled. She seems to debate with herself, torn. Then, "I think that it's a bit much. I'd have to move all my things, just to move them out again when this is all over. I have my own place, not to mention everything—my salon, my doctor, and dentist—are all local."

"You wouldn't be moving far, Melissa," I snap, "you'd still have access to your salon and whatever else you need."

"That isn't exactly the point."

I scowl too, matching Melissa's expression. I don't remember her being this stubborn, but I suppose that's what the years have done to her. Slowly, I say, "This has to be *convincing*. As I said before, you would have complete independence. I have a big penthouse with plenty of rooms, we wouldn't even have to see each other unless you wanted to. Besides, it's only temporary. Remember that."

Melissa sighs, but I can see her resolution waning. With a delicate finger pressed against her temple, she rolls her eyes. "Fine, you've convinced me," she mutters. "So long as I have my own space, and my routine doesn't change."

"Fine by me," I answer. Then, "What about your apartment? Will you end the lease?"

She looks confused, "I hadn't thought about that. It's just a rental, but..." she trails off, looking unsure.

I press on, "We need to be thorough, Melissa. If someone digs too deep, and there are holes in our story, everything falls apart."

"Of course, of course," she mutters, waving her hand dismissively. "I'll figure it out."

"And your family?" I ask, realizing we haven't broached that topic yet. "When will you tell them?"

She freezes, her expression guarded. "I'd rather not involve them in this."

Confusion creeps into my tone. "How do you expect this to be believable if no one close to you even knows we're engaged?"

"It's my family, Carter. I don't want to involve them in this lie!" she retorts, frustration evident in her voice.

We're both standing now, the tension palpable. "This needs to be genuine, Melissa! Or have you forgotten what's at stake here?"

She looks away, her face a shade redder. "I know what's at stake, but maybe you don't understand what it's like to involve your family in such a farce!"

I scoff, "You think I'm enjoying this? Deceiving everyone? I don't have a choice!"

Her voice raises, anger breaking through. "Neither do I! You think I want to tell my family that I'm engaged to some guy who doesn't even remember my name?!"

I blink. "What are you talking about? Of course, I remember your name. You're Melissa."

Her eyes widen in horror as she realizes her slip-up. "I—I meant—"

I take a step closer, studying her face. "What did you mean?"

She's silent, wringing her hands nervously. I wait, feeling a pit of dread forming in my stomach.

Taking a deep breath, she finally murmurs, "My name isn't Melissa. It's Megan."

I feel like I've been slapped. "What?"

She looks at the floor, shame evident. "Melissa is my older sister. When we were younger, you knew her, not me. I was just the younger, invisible sibling... no wonder you hardly remember me. When we met at the Vivante Grand, you thought my name was *Maggie*."

Everything suddenly clicks—the slight changes in her demeanor, the vague memories from years ago. The familiar face, yet slightly off.

"How could you lie to me?" My voice is a mixture of disbelief and anger as I stare at Megan. "Was it fun, pretending to be someone else?"

She flinches at the sharpness in my voice. "It wasn't like that, Carter," she argues defensively. "I didn't plan on it, but once the lie began, I didn't know how to stop it."

"Why not—why didn't you come clean the moment you realized I had mistaken you for Melissa?"

She meets my gaze defiantly. "Maybe because for once in my life, someone was actually seeing *me*, even if it was through the lens of being someone else. You don't know what it's like, always being in the shadow of someone else!"

I scoff, "So, your solution was to deceive me—to play a part and hope I never caught on? What were you thinking?"

Tears form in her eyes, but she blinks them away stubbornly. "I was thinking that this could be an opportunity for me. I know it was wrong, but when you proposed this whole scheme, it was as if fate was giving me a chance to step into the light, even if it was based on a lie."

I can't help the bitter laugh that escapes me. "Fate? This isn't fate, Megan. It's deception! You led me to believe I was interacting with a person from my past."

She glares at me, her chin lifting defiantly. "This is already a charade, Carter! We're planning a fake wedding! How is my lie any worse than anything else we're doing?"

"It's the principle of the matter!" I argue back. "We have a business arrangement, clear and straightforward. Now? It's muddled by your deception!"

Megan's face reddens with frustration. "You don't get it! For you, it's just a business deal, but for me, it's a chance at a better life. A chance to prove myself, to show that I am just as capable, just as deserving as Melissa. I thought... maybe in this lie, I could find some truth."

I can feel the air thick with tension, our anger and resentment unmistakable. As I look at her, the raw emotion in her eyes, something shifts inside me.

She takes a shaky breath, "Maybe we should call this off."

"You'd like that, wouldn't you? To just run away, leaving me to pick up the pieces and start all over again." My voice is cold, angry.

She meets my gaze squarely. "It's not about what I'd like. It's about what's right. If you're not comfortable, since I'm not Melissa, we can end this now."

We stare at each other, both of us teetering on the edge of a decision. After what feels like an eternity, I finally break the silence. "No, we won't end this. We'll see it through; but from now on, no more lies."

Megan nods slowly, clearly relieved. "Agreed. No more lies."

I sit back in my chair, running a hand through my hair, trying to find some semblance of composure. Megan pretending to be Melissa is a revelation that's tough to digest. But considering our current arrangement, it all feels so absurd, anyway. We're about to fake a marriage, for God's sake. What's one more lie on top of everything else?

However, things have shifted subtly. My fling with Melissa years ago was passionate and brief. She was in her last year of college, and I was finishing my MBA. Megan, Melissa's younger sister, is a faint memory from that time—a shy, overshadowed girl. But the woman in front of me now isn't that timid teenager. She's confident, determined, and unexpectedly captivating.

"We need to stay focused," I say, wanting to move past the unexpected turn our conversation has taken.

"You're right. We have to think of every detail, to make sure it's believable. If we're caught in a lie, it will be a mess for everyone."

I'm taken aback by her practical response, realizing she's as committed to this scheme as I am. "You've really thought this through."

A smile appears on her lips. "Like I said, this is a chance for a better life for me. Even if it's short-lived. Even if it began with a lie."

I study her, reflecting on how our motivations differ. For me, it's all about securing my inheritance and sidestepping my father's control. For her, this is an opportunity to emerge from someone's shadow. In a way, her clarity is something I envy.

"What about your family?" I ask. "We need to inform them, remember."

She hesitates. "They don't even know I've been seeing anyone. I'll have to think of something believable. Ideally, I wouldn't tell them at all, though."

Raising an eyebrow, I question her logic. "We've been over this—you think they won't find out? Our engagement will be public, Megan." I pause. "I was about to publicly announce my engagement to *Melissa* Medina. Wait... Why didn't my staff inform me?"

"You've always referred to me as Miss Medina to your staff. We've never been on a first name basis in front of them. They know my name is Megan."

"Crisis averted there. Now, about your family..."

She sighs, clearly conflicted. "I'll manage my family. Let's just... tackle one thing at a time."

I sense her apprehension but have my concerns to address. "Alright, fine."

We're silent for a moment, the gravity of our decision sinking in. I'm suddenly intrigued to uncover the real Megan—to understand her motivations, her aspirations, and the reasons behind such a drastic impersonation.

As Megan gathers her belongings, I notice her staring intently at the engagement ring on her finger. The sunlight from the large office windows catches the brilliant facets of the diamond, making it shimmer in a mesmerizing dance of light.

"You seem entranced," I comment with a laugh.

She looks up, seemingly caught off guard. "Oh, it's... it's just so beautiful. I've never seen anything like it."

I smirk, leaning back in my chair. "That's because not many have. It's one of a kind, just like the woman wearing it."

She raises an eyebrow, her lips curving into a sly grin. "Trying to flatter me now, Carter? Making up for the identity confusion earlier?"

"Consider it my way of extending an olive branch," I say, folding my hands behind my head, a smile tugging at my lips. "Besides, I might have a lot of money, but that doesn't mean I can't have good taste."

She laughs lightly, the tension from earlier dissipating. "Your taste in jewelry is impeccable, I'll give you that. As for your taste in women," she teases, giving me a playful wink, "I guess we'll see."

Chuckling, I say, "Well, I did choose you, didn't I?"

The lightness of our exchange is comforting, and for a fleeting moment, I believe we might genuinely get along. As with most things in life, that comfort is short-lived.

"Although," Megan starts, her tone suddenly more serious, "I'm not sure if I was chosen for the right reasons. It's all about the appearance, isn't it?"

I stiffen, her words cutting through our playful banter. "Isn't that what we both signed up for? A believable charade?"

She tilts her head, giving me a scrutinizing look. "It's just a reminder that this," she raises her hand, showcasing the ring, "as breathtaking as it is, is just another prop."

I take a deep breath, trying to control the irritation creeping into my voice. "We both know what this is, Megan. If you're having doubts—"

"I'm not," she cuts in, her gaze steady. "Let's just not pretend there isn't a person behind the role I'm playing. I hope you remember that."

I sigh, pinching the bridge of my nose. We might be more similar than I thought. Both strong-willed and unwilling to back down. "Of course I remember. You need to understand we're both making sacrifices here."

She nods, her expression softening. "Agreed. It's just a lot to take in."

As she heads for the door, I don't know how long we can maintain this ruse. Our dynamic seems extremely volatile, constantly shifting between conflict and camaraderie. One moment we're bantering, and the next, we're at each other's throats. This charade might be more challenging than either of us initially thought.

Chapter Seven

Megan

The last thing I need to be doing, after my conversation with Carter yesterday, is having dinner with my family. There's too much on my mind—and yet, this is not something I can keep putting off or work around. Carter was right, I have to tell them about our engagement.

The restaurant buzzes with the hum of conversation, the delicate clinking of silverware against plates, and the soft laughter of patrons. I fidget in my seat, scanning the menu, but the words all blur together. Across from me, after a quick update on the happenings at the biotech lab she manages, Melissa is now animatedly chatting with Mom about some new recipe she tried, her eyes bright and her laugh infectious. Dad is quietly observing the room, a faint smile on his face.

I take a shaky breath, trying to quell the swarm of butterflies in my stomach. Tonight is crucial, and I can't afford to let my nerves get the best of me.

A soft touch on my hand pulls me out of my thoughts, and I turn to see Melissa giving me a concerned look. "You okay, Megan?"

"Of course," I say as I paste on a smile. "Just... lost in thought."

Melissa studies me for a moment longer, her eyes searching my face, before she finally seems satisfied and turns her attention back to the menu.

Mom catches my gaze and tilts her head slightly, a small frown line marring her forehead. "You seem a little off tonight, dear. Is everything alright?"

I clear my throat, tucking a stray strand of hair behind my ear. "I'm fine, Mom. Just... a lot on my mind lately."

She gives me a soft smile, patting my hand. "Well, whatever it is, remember you can always talk to us."

The waiter arrives, pouring wine into our glasses. The rich, ruby-red liquid glimmers under the dim lights, and I take a tentative sip, hoping it might help calm my racing heart.

"So," Dad says, placing his menu down and looking straight at me, "why the sudden family dinner? It's not common for you to organize these things, especially at such a fancy place."

His question hangs heavily in the air. I swallow hard, feeling the pressure of their expectant eyes on me.

"Actually," I begin, my voice shaky, "there's something I do need to tell all of you."

Melissa raises an eyebrow, her interest piqued. "Sounds serious."

I glance at her. She might be my sister, and we've been through thick and thin together, but what I have to share tonight might change everything.

Dad leans back in his chair, eyeing me curiously. "Well, we're all ears, Megan."

I take another deep breath, feeling the anticipation building. This is it. The moment of truth.

The air in the room feels thick, suffocating me with a weight I can't shake off. I find myself staring into the depths of my wine glass, its rich burgundy contents swirling slowly. Taking another sip, I brace myself for the confession I'm about to make. The wine slides down smoothly, but the warmth it provides does little to calm the storm of emotions roiling within me.

Melissa, the ever persistent one, nudges my foot under the table, her eyes sharply piercing into mine. "Come on, out with it. You've got us all on edge here."

I set my glass down, taking a deep breath. "I'm engaged."
Silence.

As my words settle heavily on the table, all the chatter around us seems to fade into the background. I can feel my heart thudding against my ribcage, its rhythm echoing loudly in my ears.

Melissa's eyes widen in shock. "Wait, what? Engaged—since when?"

Dad chokes slightly on his drink, his eyes darting to Mom, who's just as surprised. "Engaged? We didn't even know you were seeing someone!"

My palms feel sweaty, and I wring my hands together under the table, trying to gather my thoughts. "It... it happened fast. Really fast. A whirlwind romance, if you will. I wanted to be sure it was serious before I involved everyone. I didn't really expect any of this when we first started dating."

Melissa's expression is a mix of disbelief and confusion. "Why wouldn't you tell me, at least? We've always shared everything."

I bite my lip, guilt gnawing at me. "I know, Melissa. I'm sorry. I just... It was so unexpected. It felt like... like I needed to protect it until I was sure it was real."

Mom reaches over, taking my hand in hers. "Oh, Megan. This is such big news. Who is he? Do we know him?"

I hesitate for a moment, then nod. "You've met him. It's Carter."

Melissa's eyebrows shoot up, her mouth forming a perfect 'O' in surprise. "Carter? As in, Carter Wright?"

Dad's gaze sharpens, and I can see the wheels turning in his head. "The billionaire? *Melissa's ex?*"

I nod again, trying to keep my voice steady. The lies are slipping past my lips a little too easily now. "Yes, that's him. I know it's a lot to take in, but... he's wonderful, and he makes me happy."

Mom's smile is warm, but there's underlying concern in her eyes. "Honey, this is huge, but I just want to be sure you're okay. That you're not rushing into anything."

I smile back, trying to reassure her. "I'm not, Mom. I promise. It's just... it's been a wild ride."

"Wild ride?" Melissa snorts, setting her glass down and folding her arms. "Megan, *wild ride* is an understatement. I mean, Carter... Seriously?"

I lean back, trying to gauge her reaction. "Yes, Carter. What's the issue?"

She raises an eyebrow, her tone dripping with skepticism. "Do you even remember how he was back when we were dating? He was all over the place, especially with the girls. Not exactly the settling-down type. It's half of why our relationship never went anywhere."

I roll my eyes, a pang of annoyance prickling at me. "Melissa, that was years ago. People change."

"Do they?" She challenges, her eyes locking on mine.

Mom intervenes, her voice soothing. "Melissa, calm down. This is Megan's decision. She's a grown woman."

Melissa exhales, frustration evident on her face. "I know, Mom, but it's my job to look out for her. You both know how Carter was when he was with me. I just... I don't want Megan to get hurt."

My heart twinges. I hadn't thought about how this would affect Melissa. Carter and her had been a fleeting thing, but it had clearly left an impression. "Melissa, I get it. It's different with us. He's been nothing but wonderful to me."

Melissa bites her lip, concern evident in her eyes. "Megan, I just want you to be cautious. He has a reputation, and not a particularly good one."

I feel a flare of defensiveness, although it's stupid. "So, what? You think he's just playing games with me?" He *is* using me, I know that, but aren't I using him too?

"No, that's not what I'm saying. I just... I know what he's like, and I don't think he's good enough for you."

My heart skips a beat. For a moment, I thought Melissa was trying to protect herself, trying to navigate her own residual feelings for Carter. It's clear now that her concern is solely for me.

"Melissa," I say, trying to convey the depth of my feelings. "I know you're worried, and I appreciate it. Carter and I, we have something real. I wouldn't have accepted his proposal if I didn't believe that."

Once again, the lie leaves a bad taste in my mouth.

She looks at me for a long moment, her expression unreadable. Then, she sighs, relenting a little. "Okay, I trust you. If he hurts you, I swear, Megan... "

I laugh, reaching over to squeeze her hand. "I know, I know."

Mom smiles, the tension in the room dissipating a little. "Girls, let's just enjoy tonight, okay? We're here to celebrate."

Melissa nods, a small smile on her lips. "You're right, Mom. I'm sorry, Megan. I just want you to be happy."

"I am happy, Melissa. Truly."

We eventually move past the initial shock, and the waiter comes around to take our orders. Dad, ever the seafood enthusiast, opts for the lobster bisque to start and a grilled salmon for the main. Melissa, going for comfort food, chooses a Caesar salad and spaghetti carbonara. Mom and I both go for the house salad, while she picks the chicken marsala and I decide on the risotto with wild mushrooms.

As the waiter leaves to put in our orders, Mom turns to me with a gleam in her eyes. "So, darling, tell us everything. How did he propose?"

My heart rate spikes. I hadn't prepared for this. What should I say? I take a deep breath, reaching for my wine glass. "Well, it was at The Imperial," I start, remembering our extravagant dinner. "We had dinner and, at the end of the meal, he just... he pulled out the ring and asked me."

Mom's eyes soften, her hand clutching her heart. "Oh, how romantic! What did he say?"

I hesitate for a split second. "He said he wanted to spend his life with me. That he couldn't imagine a future without me."

Melissa's eyes bore into mine, a flicker of doubt evident. I ignore it, focusing on the story. I'm grateful when Dad changes the subject, asking about where we're considering for the wedding venue.

Melissa's gaze returns to me, her eyes scrutinizing, searching for the truth behind my words.

It's when Mom asks about our honeymoon plans that I falter.

"Honeymoon?" I echo, my voice a little too high-pitched.

Mom nods, sipping her wine. "Yes, have you two discussed where you'll go?"

I rack my brain, trying to think of something convincing. "We haven't really decided yet. Maybe Europe? Italy, perhaps?"

Melissa's eyebrow quirks up, a knowing look in her eyes. "Italy? Carter has been there multiple times. Didn't he mention that?"

I swallow, cursing myself for the oversight. "Oh, yes. I've never been though, and he said he wouldn't mind going again if we try a new city."

It's a weak excuse, and I know it. From the corner of my eye, I can see Melissa suppressing a smirk.

Fortunately, our food arrives, breaking the tension. We dig in, the conversation shifting to lighter topics.

Throughout the meal, I feel like I'm walking a tightrope, one wrong move away from tumbling into a web of my own lies. Only Melissa seems to notice the inconsistencies in my stories. While I'm grateful for her discretion, I can't shake the feeling that she knows I'm hiding something.

The evening draws to a close, Melissa pulls me aside, her expression serious. "Megan, if there's anything you want to tell me, you can."

I give her a tight smile. "I know, Melissa. Thanks."

Melissa's green eyes mirror my own, but they're filled with a mix of concern and determination that makes my stomach churn with anxiety. For a moment, I think about admitting everything, pouring out the whole absurd story to her. Before I can decide how to proceed, the honking of a taxi interrupts our stand-off.

"We've found a taxi!" Dad shouts, motioning for us to hurry over.

Melissa's gaze doesn't waver, and she takes a deep breath as if to say something more, but she's interrupted by Mom's voice echoing our dad's sentiment. "Come along, girls!"

"Melissa," I start, but she lifts a hand to halt my words.

"We'll talk later," she promises, her gaze heavy and unreadable.

We rush over to where our parents are waiting, and I'm grateful for the temporary reprieve, even though I know it won't last. The taxi ride is silent for the most part, save for Dad's occasional comments about the city or Mom's gentle chatter about her garden club and friends. Melissa and I sit on opposite ends, our silence a palpable tension in the confined space of the car.

As we pull up to our childhood home, a quaint two-story house with faded red bricks and ivy climbing the sides, I'm reminded of simpler times when my biggest worry was getting home before curfew or an upcoming exam. That feels like a lifetime ago now.

Mom is the first to break the silence once we step out of the car. "Why don't you girls come inside for a nightcap? We have that nice bottle of wine Melissa brought last Christmas."

"That sounds lovely," Melissa agrees, her tone polite but distant. The undercurrent of tension between us hasn't gone unnoticed.

"I'd love to," I say, hoping the added time might help me figure out how to handle this situation, and feel out Melissa's perspective.

Once inside, the familiarity of our childhood home surrounds me—the scent of Mom's freshly baked cookies, the worn-out carpet that's seen better days, and the family photos that line the walls. But instead of offering comfort, they only amplify my guilt.

We settle in the living room, and as Mom pours the wine, Melissa's gaze meets mine across the room. It's clear she's waiting, biding her time for a chance to talk to me alone.

After what feels like hours but is probably only minutes, I finally find my voice. "Melissa, I promise, everything is fine."

She looks at me, clearly skeptical. "Is it? Because from where I'm sitting, it looks like you're in over your head."

I wince, knowing she's right, but not ready to admit it. Before I can craft a response, our parents re-enter the room, bringing with them a reprieve from our conversation. The silent promise between Melissa and I remains, hovering in the air, a reminder of the storm that's yet to come.

Chapter Eight

Megan

The allure of the Fitzgerald Hotel's lavish interior always takes my breath away. Gilded ceilings and marble pillars set the scene for one of the city's most prestigious networking events. As I walk in, the weight of the golden chandelier above and the soft, ambient lighting make it clear that this isn't just any ordinary venue. I'm surrounded by the city's business elite, all dressed to the nines, exchanging pleasantries and deals in the same breath.

Every conversation is a dance, an art form that requires grace, timing, and finesse. I move through the crowd, offering smiles and pleasantries, engaging in light chit-chat with potential partners.

"Miss Medina?" A young woman in a sleek black dress stops me, holding out her card. "A pleasure to meet you. I've heard a lot about your consultancy—*and* your engagement to Mr. Wright... two, three days ago?"

I wince as I take her card and reply, "Thank you. It's always wonderful to meet new faces." We chat for a few minutes, and to my chagrin, talk turns to my engagement instead of my career.

"Mr. Wright's hotels are so beautiful. Maybe even more so than the Fitzgerald. Tell me, have you set a date for the wedding?"

I flush but meet her gaze head on. "No, we haven't set a date yet. Here's my business card."

"Surely you shouldn't be working still? You're engaged to a *billionaire!* You'll never need to work another day in your life."

"Yes, well, I quite enjoy my work. I wouldn't want to sit around bored all day."

"And what does he think of that?"

Great. Just what I need. After managing to avoid the press for so long, *this* is what's going to make me lose my temper. As calmly as possible, I say, "Carter is happy for me to continue my business. He's a businessman himself, he understands the virtue of hard work and keeping busy."

Even the suggestion that he's so kindly *allowed* me to keep working makes my skin crawl. It seems to satisfy her though, as she nods and moves on to the next person. For now, I'm safe.

I find someone else to chat with, handing out business cards to anyone who seems interested. I repeat this ritual several times, the stack of my own business cards slowly dwindling as the night goes on. As always with these events, I find the need for a brief respite to breathe and recalibrate.

Stepping out into the cool evening air on the hotel's balcony, I take a moment to admire the cityscape below, the distant lights shimmering like stars. My brief peace is interrupted by a deep, stern voice.

"You're treading on dangerous ground, Miss Medina."

Startled, I turn to face the source. A stocky man with graying hair stands a few steps away, his features set in a scowl. His sharp suit screams power, and there's an aura of intensity about him.

"I'm sorry, have we met?" I say, trying to mask the unease that tightens around my chest.

He steps closer, his gaze unwavering. "No, but I know of you, and more importantly, I know of your... fiancé."

The emphasis on *fiancé* makes it clear he isn't just another potential business partner. My mind races. Why is Carter's name a factor in this? And then it dawns on me. "You're Josh Warrington, aren't you?"

His lips curl into a smirk, the grim expression on his face barely lifting. "So, you've heard of me."

"Well, you *do* own this hotel," I say defensively. Why is one of the city's most influential businessmen confronting me on a balcony?

He circles me, making it clear he's the predator and I'm the prey. "You're playing a dangerous game aligning yourself with Carter. This is my territory, and I don't take kindly to encroachments."

Feeling cornered, my pulse quickens. "I'm just here for the networking, Mr. Warrington. I have no business disputes with you."

He leans in, his voice low and threatening. "Just remember, alliances have consequences, Miss Medina. It would be a shame if your business met with... unforeseen obstacles."

Taking a deep breath, I attempt to square my shoulders and find some semblance of the confidence I usually exude. "I don't appreciate threats, Mr. Warrington," I begin, my voice wavering slightly despite my efforts to remain firm.

He glances at me with a mixture of amusement and condescension. "You think you're in a position to dictate terms?"

"I don't understand why you're making this personal. What have I, or even Carter, done to offend you to such a degree?"

I question, genuinely trying to wrap my head around the situation.

He pauses for a moment, studying me. "You really don't know, do you? Carter and I... " He practically spits the name out, "what we have is more than just a personal affair."

"Then enlighten me," I challenge, taking a step forward.

He tilts his head, observing me with a newfound curiosity. "You're brave. I'll give you that. It's not bravery that keeps one afloat in the business world. It's ruthlessness."

I narrow my eyes, my patience waning. "What's your issue with Carter?"

Josh sighs deeply, as if I'm a child who just asked a profoundly naïve question. "It's not just one issue. Business between our families goes back generations. Loyalties, betrayals, mergers, and backstabs—it's all a game. Carter and I are just the current players. And Carter, well, Carter comes out on the winning side too often. Just hard, smart work? I don't think so."

"Where do I fit in this game?" I ask, trying to keep my voice steady.

His smirk returns, cold and mocking. "Maybe you're a pawn, maybe a queen. That's for you to decide. Even queens can be dethroned."

I swallow hard, a chill running down my spine. "I'm not afraid of you," I say, mustering up as much defiance as I can.

Josh leans down, his face inches from mine. His hazel eyes are piercing, demanding my full attention. "You should be," he whispers.

He straightens up and glances at the door leading back to the event. "Learn the rules of the game, Megan. Play it well. Otherwise, you'll find yourself checkmated before you even know what hit you."

With that cryptic warning, he strides off, disappearing into the night. As I'm left standing there, my mind racing, trying to process the encounter. The cold air bites at my skin, but it's Josh's words that send shivers down my spine.

Shaking off the unease, I push open the grand doors and step back into the warm embrace of the Fitzgerald Hotel's ballroom. Scanning the room, I try to locate Josh, but he's nowhere to be found. It's as if he's vanished, leaving only the echo of his threats behind.

The warmth of the ballroom embraces me, the rich music and sounds of clinking glasses acting as a balm after the unsettling encounter with Josh Warrington. I head toward the bar, trying to shake off the sense of unease.

"Evening, ma'am. What can I get for you?" the bartender asks, polishing a glass.

"A white wine, please," I respond, attempting to regain my composure.

As I wait for my drink, I unzip my purse and pull out my neatly stacked business cards. It's always a good idea to be prepared at these types of events. As I flick through them, however, I come across a card that certainly isn't mine.

It's crisp, sleek, and black with silver embossing:

Josh WarringtonCEO of Warrington Group Hotels

I stare at the card, a sense of dread settling in my stomach. When did he manage to slip it into my purse? Was it a message, or a challenge? Or perhaps just another game in the world of high stakes business.

Regardless of his intent, it rattles me. The sheer audacity of the gesture, the invasion of my personal space... it's unsettling. For a fleeting moment, I feel out of my depth.

My fingers play with the edges of the card, contemplating tossing it. Something stops me. Instead, I tuck it behind my cards—hidden, but not discarded.

"Here you are," the bartender says, handing me my drink. I nod in appreciation, taking a sip of the cool, crisp wine. It's just what I need.

Lost in thought, I'm jolted back to the present by a familiar voice. "Megan! I didn't expect to see you here!"

I turn to see Tim Donnelly, his awkward smile breaking into a grin. I can't say I'm glad to see him, but a familiar face is somewhat appreciated.

"Tim! What brings you here?" I ask, managing a weak smile.

He chuckles. "Oh, I just wanted to see what the competition's offering. I must admit, this place gives the Vivante Grand a run for its money."

"Really?" I say, raising an eyebrow. "Better than the Vivante Grand? That's a bold statement."

Tim shrugs, leaning against the bar. "I believe in giving credit where credit's due. This place is something. The ambience, the decor... it's impressive. But," he winks, "it doesn't have you, so the Vivante Grand still holds an edge."

I laugh, the tension from earlier easing a little. "You know I don't actually work at the Vivante Grand, right?"

He raises his glass in a mock toast. "Yeah, but you've been there so much lately it's starting to feel like it."

Tim's smile never wavers, but I've always found something slightly off-putting about it. It's just a touch too bright, a little too persistent. Since my very first business meeting at the Vivante Grand, Tim has made it evident that his interest in me wasn't just professional. I, on the other hand, have always tried to maintain a clear boundary, though it isn't always easy with someone as persistently friendly as Tim.

"So, Megan," he starts, swirling the dark liquid in his glass, "How are your latest clients doing? Any big projects coming up?"

Grateful for the change in topic, I smile genuinely this time. "Oh, Miss Barker and Mr. Davis are wonderful. They're deep into planning their wedding. It's always nice to be a part of someone's special day."

Tim's eyes brighten, "They're always a joyous occasion. Must be a treat working with happy couples all the time."

"It is. Though sometimes the planning can be... intense. It's so rewarding, though."

Tim nods, seemingly lost in thought. After a brief pause, he says, "I remember you once said what you loved most about weddings. The whole fairy-tale aspect of it. It must be dreamy to be part of that process."

I roll my eyes, "Yes, I did say that. You remember the oddest things, Tim."

He shrugs, the ever-present smile never leaving his face, "I remember things about people who matter."

I'm saved from responding by the arrival of another guest who greets Tim with familiarity. They delve into a conversation about a mutual project, and I use the moment to glance around the ballroom.

The music swells, and I see couples dancing. It's a beautiful sight, and I imagine what it'd be like to have Carter here with me. Even though our engagement is nothing more than a charade, the thought brings a warmth to my cheeks.

After a while, I turn back to Tim, who seems to have wrapped up his conversation. He's looking at me with that same intent gaze, making me slightly uncomfortable. "You seem miles away," he says.

"Just lost in thought."

Tim's gaze sharpens a bit, "About the couple you're planning the wedding for?"

I nod, eager to shift the conversation back to neutral ground. "Yes, they're a unique pair. Quite the challenge, but it's been fun."

"Good to hear." There's a pause. "You deserve all the happiness in the world, Megan."

It's meant to be a kind statement, but something in his tone makes me uneasy. I'm just about to respond when my phone buzzes in my purse. Using it as an excuse, I bid Tim a quick goodbye, relieved to have a reason to escape.

As I walk away, I feel Tim's gaze on my back. The evening was supposed to be about networking, but now, all I want is to be somewhere safe, away from the prying eyes and unsolicited attention.

Chapter Nine

Carter

Entering the Vivante Grand always gives me a nostalgic thrill. The grand chandeliers, the plush red carpets—every detail brings back memories. Of all the hotels I've seen and managed, the Vivante Grand remains close to my heart. It was where I cut my teeth in the business, where I found my footing.

My father has just answered the phone after calling to tell him about my new engagement. I tell him the news through pursed lips as I pray he won't dig too deep into the lies.

"This is... unexpected," my father admits. In the background, I can hear the beeping of a heart monitor. "I must admit though, I'm proud. I know what you're capable of when you put your mind to it."

"Thank you, Father. Now if you'll excuse me..."

"Yes, yes, you're a busy man. Get back to work, then."

I hang up with little fanfare, relief settling in my stomach. I wander up to the reception desk with an easy smile.

"Mr. Wright!" Laura, my loyal receptionist, greets me with her ever-present warmth. "Didn't expect to see you today."

"I had some time, Laura. Thought I'd see how our flagship hotel is doing."

She chuckles, "Still standing tall and proud, just like always. Especially with you leading the charge now."

As we chat, my gaze drifts past the desk, landing on Tim Donnelly. He's trying to be discreet, but it's obvious he's eavesdropping on our conversation. Particularly when Megan's name is mentioned.

Laura, ever observant, catches my drift. "Mr. Donnelly seems to have developed quite an interest in your... fiancée," she murmurs.

I raise an eyebrow. "Is that so?"

She nods, her expression a mix of amusement and caution. "He's quite smitten. Though I don't know if that's good for Megan."

I can't help the surge of possessiveness that bubbles up. "She's engaged. He should remember that."

Laura smirks, "A little piece of metal never stopped Tim before."

The implications of our charade suddenly feel more complex. I'm acting a part, but some of these emotions feel all too real.

Before I can process my thoughts further, Tim approaches with that trademark grin on his face.

"Mr. Wright," he greets, his voice dripping with false warmth. "Didn't expect you here."

"Tim." I say, forcing politeness. "Just touring the Grand."

His eyes glint with mischief. "And how's Megan? I saw her at the Fitzgerald on Friday."

"She's well, thanks for asking," I answer, keeping my voice even, though I'd love to wipe that smirk off his face. "Although, I have to wonder what you were doing at a rival hotel."

He nods, but there's something in his gaze that rubs me the wrong way. He avoids mention of the Fitzgerald by saying, "Megan's a real catch, Mr. Wright. You're one lucky man."

I stare him down, my voice firm. "I know."

There's clear tension between us. Finally, he breaks it, nodding curtly. "If you need anything, just give a shout."

Watching him walk away, unease settles in my chest. It's clear there's more at play than I initially thought. If I'm not careful, things could get messy between us and Megan.

I refocus on Laura, noticing the lines of irritation marring her usually collected face. "That man truly has a gift for not knowing when to shut up," she mutters.

I chuckle, though there's no real humor behind it. "That might be the understatement of the year."

Laura shakes her head, her smile apologetic. "I'm sorry about all of this, Mr. Wright. Tim is a nice enough man, just nosy."

I nod, my mind still churning with all the new information. "Thank you, Laura. It's not your fault. People will do what they like, I suppose."

She offers a sympathetic smile. "At least you're used to it. It's part and parcel of being a Wright."

I run a hand through my hair. "That doesn't mean I have to like it."

We exchange a few more pleasantries before I excuse myself, needing a moment to collect my thoughts. I make my way to the bar, the idea of a strong coffee to help clear my mind pulling me forward. There's a quiet hum of activity as patrons chat and workers move about their duties.

Approaching the bar, I overhear the two bartenders in hushed conversation. Their words catch my attention instantly.

"... heard it from Wanda. She said Mr. Wright's been seen out with some other woman. His poor fiancée is gonna be heartbroken."

The other man whistles, low and impressed. "Man, if it's true, that's bold even for him. An engagement's one thing, but cheating?"

My blood boils. Not only are there rumors, but they're about me cheating? This is absurd. It takes all my restraint to keep from confronting them right there. I take a deep breath, reminding myself that scenes are counterproductive, especially in my position.

I clear my throat loudly, causing both men to jump. They flush as they realize they've been overheard, and I can see the guilt in their eyes.

"Gentlemen," I start, my voice cold. "If I were you, I'd be more careful about what I say, and especially about whom I say it. Rumors can be harmful."

They both stammer out apologies, tripping over their words in their haste to backtrack. I merely nod, keeping my expression impassive.

"And, for the record," I continue, leaning in slightly, "I'd appreciate it if you'd refrain from speculating about my personal life. If I wanted the staff to know, I'd tell them myself."

The two of them nod, eyes wide, and I can only hope the message sticks. I take my coffee to go, needing some fresh air and space to process everything. This charade with Megan was supposed to solve my problems, not complicate them further.

The Vivante Grand's courtyard has always been an oasis of calm for me, a stark contrast to the hustle and bustle of the hotel's interior. Today, as I step out into its welcoming embrace, I'm greeted by the soothing sound of water trickling from a stone fountain at its center. White marble paths meander through meticulously manicured gardens, leading guests to secluded seating areas where they can enjoy their privacy. A few early evening guests stroll around leisurely, their voices hushed in reverence to the serenity of the place. The golden hues of the setting sun filter through the leafy canopies overhead, casting dappled patterns on the ground below.

I find a quiet spot on a stone bench, partially obscured by a fragrant jasmine bush, and sit down. The sheer beauty of the courtyard offers some solace, and my racing heart begins to slow. Yet, the rumors, the deceit, and the uncertainty of where the lies are coming from taints the peace I usually find here.

As I sip the bitter coffee, I find my thoughts drifting to Tim. Would he be willing to spread such rumors? Jealousy can make people do unthinkable things, and I've seen firsthand the way he looks at Megan. Even so, would he stoop so low and risk his position? He's always struck me as a bit strange, but never malicious.

Then again, the Vivante Group is a hive of ambition, competition, and intrigue. Could it be someone else with a vendetta against me, using the rumors as a weapon? Perhaps someone I'd inadvertently sidelined in my climb to the top, or someone who saw an advantage to sullying my reputation?

The questions swirl endlessly, offering no answers. It's exhausting, this constant second-guessing, the never-ending dance of deceit and false appearances. What started as a seemingly simple charade with Megan is snowballing into a nightmare of complications. With each passing day, the lines between reality and pretense blur a little more.

A soft rustling sound to my right snaps me out of my reverie. I turn to see a familiar figure approaching. It's Megan, her face a mask of concern. She must've heard about the rumors, I realize. For a moment, I'm torn between relief at seeing her and a fresh surge of anger at the situation we find ourselves in.

"Megan," I greet, my voice strained.

She stops a few feet away, her gaze searching mine. "Carter, I heard some... whispers about us while I was with my client, Miss Barker."

I nod, not trusting my voice.

She hesitates for a moment, her fingers playing with the edge of her purse. "Who would do this?"

I let out a humorless chuckle. "The Vivante Grand has no shortage of potential culprits. Don't worry, I'll get to the bottom of this."

She takes a seat next to me, our shoulders touching lightly. The closeness is comforting, even in the midst of this storm. We sit in silence, lost in our thoughts, drawing strength from each other's presence.

Megan's fingers slide into mine, a tentative gesture that sends a jolt of warmth up my arm. It's familiar by now—this playacting, these rehearsed displays of affection—but tonight, it feels different. As her thumb brushes over the back of my hand, I find myself pulling her closer, compelled by an urge I can't quite put my finger on.

It's almost reflexive, the way I tilt her chin up and press a gentle kiss to her forehead. She leans into the touch, the soft curve of her face fitting perfectly under my lips. My chest constricts at the proximity, at the intimacy of the moment. The line between what's real and what's not seems to blur for a few seconds.

There's a silent, lingering tension between us—an intense energy. I wonder if she feels it too. I fight the urge to close the gap between us, to give in to the growing attraction. *She's not really my fiancée,* I remind myself. This is all pretend. Still, my heart refuses to listen, its rhythm betraying the conflict raging within.

It's Megan who breaks the silence, her voice soft yet hesitant. "Carter... about Tim. He was at the Fitzgerald Hotel when I was there. He was... off. Almost too interested in what I was doing, and he mentioned the Vivante a couple of times. I didn't think much of it at the time, but now... "

I frown, her words echoing my own suspicions. "What did he say?"

She shrugs, her fingers tracing patterns on the back of my hand. "Nothing outright suspicious. Just asking about my clients, and that he liked seeing me around the Vivante... but there was something in his eyes. It's hard to explain."

A shiver of unease runs down my spine. If Tim is somehow involved, it complicates matters even more. With the rumors circulating, it's not outside the realm of possibility.

"I thought I was overthinking things," Megan continues, "but seeing how he's acting here... Carter, do you think he could be behind the rumors?"

I let out a sigh, my thoughts a tangled mess. "I don't want to point fingers without proof, but... it wouldn't surprise me. Laura's trustworthy, and I don't trade in gossip but she says he's been a bit too nosy. What's he got to gain from it, though?"

Megan pulls away slightly, her gaze distant. "I don't know. Whatever it is, we need to be careful. If he's trying to sabotage us, he might have other plans too."

I nod in agreement. The idea of Tim—or anyone else, for that matter—trying to ruin what we've built, even if it's based on a lie, angers me more than I care to admit.

"We'll figure it out," I say, squeezing her hand reassuringly.

She smiles weakly, her gaze meeting mine. Amidst the chaos and uncertainty, I'm struck by a startling realization. While our relationship may have started as a ruse, the connection, the bond forming between us, is anything but fake.

Chapter Ten

Megan

The world outside shifts in hues of oranges and purples as the day slowly descends into twilight. I glance at Carter as we leave the hotel. He seems more at ease than I've ever seen him, and a part of me wonders if it's an act. Does he ever let his guard down? Or is this serene look just another part of the façade?

He leads the way into the restaurant—another towering, gleaming establishment that screams opulence. Crystal chandeliers hang overhead, shimmering in the soft glow of the dwindling evening light. Rich, velvet drapes frame vast windows overlooking the bustling city streets. It's breathtaking.

"Ever been here before?" he asks, guiding me to a cozy corner table, its surface polished to a mirror-like finish.

"No," I reply, glancing around. "It's beautiful."

His lips quirk up. "I thought you'd like it."

A server promptly appears, greeting Carter like an old friend. "Mr. Wright, always a pleasure."

Carter nods politely. "Likewise. We'll start with two glasses of your finest champagne."

The server bows and slips away, leaving us alone in our corner. I feel Carter's gaze on me. I meet it, my heart rate quickening. There's an intensity in his eyes that I haven't seen before, and it takes me off guard.

"You okay?" he asks, leaning slightly forward.

I nod, smiling. "Just thinking how different this is from our usual meetings."

His mouth quirks. "Is that a bad thing?"

"No," I say, "It's nice."

There's a momentary silence, broken only by the soft hum of conversations around us. I take a moment to soak it all in. The plush seating, the faint clinking of glasses, the luxurious ambiance—it's surreal.

Our drinks arrive, and I pick up my glass, the cold condensation tickling my fingers. "To... us?" I propose, amusement in my voice.

Carter chuckles, clinking his glass against mine. "To us."

The champagne is crisp and bubbly, the taste dancing on my tongue. Our conversation flows with surprising ease. We talk about everything and nothing—favorite movies, travel experiences, future plans. It's light and carefree, a sharp contrast to our usual heavy discussions.

I notice the glances thrown our way—whispers and subtle nods from the other patrons. It dawns on me that Carter likely chose this place not just for its ambiance but for its public nature. A couple of glances, a few whispers, and our charade would be solidified in the eyes of many. It's a brilliant move, and I admire his foresight.

Yet, despite the pretense, there's a warmth in his voice, a softness in his gaze that seems genuine. Every time our hands brush, every shared laugh, every whispered secret, blurs the line between what's real and what's not.

The dimmed atmosphere of the restaurant creates an intimacy that's hard to deny. The soft music playing in the background is the perfect accompaniment to the deepening connection between Carter and I. My thoughts drift, wandering into uncharted territory as the warm glow from our drinks envelope me.

"Why did you choose this place?" I ask, tracing the rim of my glass with a finger, watching the play of lights against the liquid inside.

Carter looks up, a slow smile forming. "I haven't been here in a long while, I thought it would be nice to go somewhere *other* than the same three places I always go. You know, step out of the box a little."

I chuckle. "The Vivante Grand isn't enough of a box for you?"

He laughs, shaking his head. "Sometimes it's good to escape, even if just for a little while."

Our gazes lock, and there's an electric charge in the air. Something shifts, becoming more tangible. I take a deep breath, my heart racing, and lean forward so far that our noses brush.

He leans into me, his voice dropping to a huskier tone. "You know, you're full of surprises, Megan."

"Am I?" My voice is breathless, the world around us fading. There's only Carter and the pounding of my heartbeat in my ears.

His eyes darken, his gaze dropping to my lips. "You have no idea," he whispers, and that's all the encouragement I need. Closing the gap between us, our lips meet. The kiss starts off tentatively, a soft brush of lips—a play, part of our act. Within seconds, it deepens, becomes more passionate, the boundary between reality and pretense dissolving.

His hands come up to cup my face, tilting my head just right as the world falls away. The taste of him—champagne and warmth—fills my senses. Everything feels magnified—the pressure of his lips, the heat of his touch, the fluttering in my stomach.

When we finally pull apart, both of us are breathing heavily. Carter's eyes are filled with a warmth that makes my heart skip a beat. Before I can find my voice, he's grinning, with that mischievous spark back in his eyes.

I blink, slightly dazed. "What was that for?"

His grin widens. "Just wanted to see if the reality lived up to the hype."

Laughing, I shake my head. "And?"

He pretends to think for a moment, tapping his chin. "I think I might need more data to be sure." With that, he pulls me closer, wrapping an arm around my waist. I barely have time to catch my breath before his lips are on mine again.

This kiss is different—more intense, more demanding. It's a claiming, and I find myself willingly lost in the lust he invokes. By the time we pull apart, I'm breathless and giddy, the world spinning slightly.

We lean back in the booth, the lingering effects of our kissing illuminating both of our faces. For the first time, I feel a genuine connection with Carter—a raw, genuine attraction that can't be scripted or faked.

The night air is cool and refreshing as we exit the restaurant. That chill is immediately forgotten as Carter suddenly stops, turning to face me with an intensity that makes my breath catch. In one fluid motion, he pulls me into him. The electric charge forming between us is escalating.

His gaze never leaves mine as he slowly leans down, capturing my lips with his. The kiss is fierce and demanding, sending shivers down my spine. Before I have time to process what's happening between us, he's pushing me gently against his sleek car, the cold metal a stark contrast to the warmth of his body pressing against mine.

His lips move from my mouth to the curve of my neck, sending waves of pleasure through me with every pull. My fingers weave into his hair, pulling him closer, urging him on. With a soft growl, his hands start to explore, skimming over my waist and slowly gliding up my skirt.

A jolt of desire courses through me as his fingers sneak past my thin panties. It's a gentle yet assertive touch, a tease that promises so much more. The first finger slides inside of me and I stifle a gasp. "Here?" I murmur, but my complaint dies as Carter begins to work me with a slow, even pump of his wrist.

I tilt my head, giving him better access, thighs spread as my own hands explore the muscular contours of his back through his shirt. He's both gentle and insistent, making my heart race and my thoughts scatter with desire.

For a moment, all worries, all pretenses, disappear. The lines between our charade and the genuine desire growing between us fade even more, and the world with all the doubts that come with it melts away. He quickens his pace, breath hot against my neck and I groan, my head tipping back against the car as I no longer have the strength to hold it upright.

Breathing heavily, he pulls back slightly, his eyes searching mine. The vulnerability in his gaze surprises me. "Megan," he whispers, his voice filled with a mix of desire and something deeper, something I can't quite place.

I swallow hard, equally affected. "Carter," I murmur.

My fingers trace the line of his jaw, and his grip tightens around me. The world around us fades, and I come around his fingers with a muffled cry. I bury my face into his neck as my orgasm shakes me, eyes scrunched shut. I'm dizzy from the force of it.

He seems to lose himself as well, and for a second, I fear we'll get caught. The risk, the danger, it all adds to the electric charge between us. Then I remember where we are, in a public parking lot, and I force myself to suppress the soft sounds threatening to escape my lips.

Finally, after what feels like an eternity but is probably only minutes, Carter releases me. I take a deep breath, trying to steady my racing heart, and grin up at him. There's a twinkle in his eye, an unspoken acknowledgment of our shared moment.

Wordlessly, I adjust my skirt and give him a playful peck on the lips. With a chivalrous gesture, he opens the car door for me. I slide in, feeling the cool plush leather against my flushed skin, and he swiftly takes his place behind the wheel.

Once we're on the road, Carter lets out a low chuckle, breaking the silence. "That was... unexpectedly impulsive," he says, shooting me a sidelong glance. His cheeks are flushed, and there's a wild sparkle in his eyes.

I laugh, my earlier nervousness replaced by a giddy feeling. "You don't say, but I didn't hear you complaining."

He smirks. "I'd be lying if I said I regretted it. Though we should probably be more careful."

The car glides smoothly through the city streets, the soft hum of the engine blending with the quiet tunes playing on the radio. For a while, we drive in comfortable silence, lost in our thoughts.

The city lights play a mesmerizing dance outside the windows, casting ever-changing shadows across the car's interior. My mind races, trying to process what just happened. Are we still playing a game? Or is this becoming something more real?

The city lights streak past in a blur, each one a fleeting moment. I hear Carter take a deep breath beside me, but he doesn't speak immediately. We both seem trapped in our own thoughts, the silence in the car growing heavier with each passing second.

It's Carter who breaks the quiet, though not in the direction I expected. "How are things going with your clients? Miss Barker and Mr. Davis, I mean."

I'm momentarily stunned speechless by the change in topic, my mind grappling to find the appropriate details. I take a deep breath and nod, "Yes, they've finally settled on a date for their reception at The Vivante Grand. They're really excited."

"That's great to hear," he replies, his tone genuine, but my mind isn't fully on the current conversation. Every fiber of my being wants to circle back to the unspoken words, the unaddressed emotions between us. However, the fear of ruining what we have, even if it's just a charade, stops me.

Carter seems to sense my distraction, but he doesn't push. "The Vivante Grand is the perfect choice," he continues, smoothly switching back to professional mode. "It's one of my favorites. Did you know that I was an events organizer there, before taking over as the CEO?"

The car weaves through the streets, and I find myself studying Carter's profile. Even in the dim light, his features are strikingly handsome, and I'm caught off guard by a pang of desire. The kiss, the touch, the unspoken connection—it's all so fresh in my memory, distracting me from his words. Yet, here he is, discussing work as if nothing happened.

Wanting to keep the conversation light, I respond, "I can see why it holds a special place in your heart."

He nods. "Indeed. It's where it all began for me."

The conversation drifts to more mundane topics as we continue our drive. Carter talks about some of the challenges he faced when taking over The Vivante Grand and his plans for the future. I listen, but my heart isn't in it. I'm too wrapped up in my own thoughts, and the fear of what might happen if I address the growing tension between us.

Before I know it, we're pulling up outside my building. Carter turns off the engine, the soft hum coming to a halt. We sit there for a moment, neither of us making a move.

Finally, I break the silence, "Thank you for the evening, Carter. It was... unexpected."

He chuckles softly, "In more ways than one." His gaze lingers on mine, searching, questioning. Neither of us speaks the words that hang in the air between us.

With a final nod, I step out of the car, feeling the unspoken emotions spinning in my mind. As I make my way to my apartment building, I wonder if things between Carter and I have changed forever.

Chapter Eleven

Carter

Watching Megan exit the car, I'm caught within a myriad of emotions. The evening had turned out far more intense than I'd anticipated, and the boundaries between our charade and reality are crumbling.

She pauses for a moment, fumbling with her cellphone. She turns back after a second. "Carter," she says, and there's an edge to her voice. "Is it just me, or was tonight *actually* quite fun?"

I stiffen, my defenses shooting up. "Megan," I say, as I lean out of the car window. "No need to ruin a good night. We both know this isn't real."

She pivots to face me, hurt evident in her gaze. "I know but... never mind. Forget I said anything."

"No, finish that thought."

Megan scowls. "Tonight was... unexpected. I enjoyed it, and I wonder if that's a good thing or not. It doesn't matter. Like I said, forget it. I just didn't expect it to go so well. That's all."

"Try not to have too much fun," I quip, "or you'll forget where we stand."

Her eyes flash with a mix of anger and sadness. "So I'm not allowed to have fun? If we're putting so much effort into faking this, it should at least be enjoyable."

"You know it's more complicated than that," I retort. "Let's not lose sight of why we started this charade."

"You're unbelievable, Carter. I thought maybe for once we'd be able to agree."

"This isn't about having *fun*. It's about keeping a promise. You know why I'm doing this."

"Really? Then what was *that* in the parking lot?"

A tense silence ensues. Her words hang heavily in the air. I want to bridge the gap between us, but my own fears and past mistakes hold me back. "Megan, I—"

She cuts me off, her voice determined. "It's clear where you stand, Carter, but it takes two to play this game. Right now, you're making it very difficult."

We're locked in a silent standoff, two souls at odds.

I clench my jaw, holding back the torrent of emotions threatening to break free. "Megan, let's not make this personal. I've been upfront about my intentions from the start."

She scoffs, "Have you? Because it sure as hell seems like you're sending mixed signals. One moment you're seemingly into me, and the next you're trying your hardest to start a fight with me."

"I'm trying to maintain the boundaries we put in place," I respond tersely.

"You can't keep using that as an excuse, Carter. A bit of fun is hardly breaking the rules."

"I won't let things get muddled," I fire back. "Maybe if you hadn't started this whole thing under false pretenses, things would be clearer."

"Are you seriously bringing that up now? How is that even relevant?"

"How is it relevant? Megan, you literally pretended to be someone else. That's not just some minor detail. It speaks to trust, or a lack thereof."

She points a finger at me accusingly. "You're using that as a diversion. This argument isn't about that. It's about you being a damn coward."

I raise an eyebrow, offended. "A coward, really? You sure have a way of turning things around, don't you?"

"Maybe you're just afraid of us having fun because you think it will become too real. Now you have the audacity to bring up my past mistake?"

"You're making this about us, Megan. I'm reminding you of facts. You started this relationship on a lie."

She takes a shaky breath, trying to calm herself. "Yes, I made a mistake, and I've apologized for it. You don't get to use it as a weapon against me now."

I shake my head, exasperated. "You're missing the point. It's about trust, Megan. If you could pretend to be Melissa, who's to say you're not pretending now? Maybe *you're* the one who wants more."

The hurt in her eyes is clear, but she doesn't waver. "You don't know me at all, Carter."

I feel a pang of guilt but push it aside. "Maybe you don't know me either. If you did, you'd know I've no interest in *fun*."

"So what now, we just call it quits?"

I exhale slowly. "Maybe we should. Maybe this whole thing was a mistake."

My chest rises and falls rapidly, my anger still raw in the stillness of the night. I turn my head slightly, watching Megan's face, a mixture of hurt and defiance. The tension between us is like a taut line, threatening to snap.

"It was never supposed to get this complicated," I finally admit, my voice rough.

Megan's eyes flash with pain. "That's just it, isn't it? You wanted a convenient facade. Things are never that simple. We

87

don't have to agree on everything, but God, stop starting a fight over a silly comment about enjoying our time together."

I shake my head, my frustration building. "This is about the inheritance, about securing my future after my father... " I trail off, unwilling to delve into that fresh wound.

"You can't use your father's condition as an excuse," she retorts bitterly. "It's all right to enjoy yourself. If anything, it makes this look more real."

My mind races, feelings and logic clashing inside. "Of course this is about the inheritance. Everything else is just acting."

"Yeah, sure," Megan snaps, her eyes watery but fierce. "I just don't understand why this whole thing has to be miserable for us both. We enjoy spending time together—why does that have to be a bad thing?"

I groan in frustration, running a hand through my hair. "Megan, that's exactly why we should've kept things clear. We knew the boundaries. We set them ourselves."

She tilts her head, her voice softer but filled with sorrow. "What if those boundaries change, Carter—does it scare you so much that we might actually get along?"

My chest tightens at her words. The truth is, it does scare me. I've been hurt in the past, and the idea of opening myself up again, especially under such unusual circumstances, terrifies me. I can't admit that to her. Not now.

"It doesn't matter," I say, trying to regain my composure. "The parameters were clear. If you've let yourself feel more, that's on you."

The hurt in her eyes deepens, and for a split second, I think she's going to break down right then and there, but Megan is stronger than that. Instead, she straightens up, her chin lifted defiantly.

"Hey now, I never said anything about *feelings*," she says curtly. "I get it. You don't want to risk anything real, anything substantial, but that's never going to happen. You're just like your father, thinking you're so above everyone else."

That comment hits me like a ton of bricks, and my voice drops dangerously low. "Don't bring him into this."

She just shakes her head, a mirthless smile curving at her lips. "Goodnight, Carter." Without another word, she pivots on her heel and walks away, leaving me alone with my thoughts, and regrets.

I watch her receding figure, our words hanging heavily in the air. As the distance between us grows, I can't shake the feeling that we've crossed a point of no return.

The world seems to have blended into indistinct shapes and colors, leaving me with only the stark image of Megan's retreating form. I find myself gripping the steering wheel so tightly my knuckles turn white. As the engine hums to life, the gentle vibration does little to quell the storm of emotions raging within me.

Megan's last words echo in my mind. Every inflection, every ounce of hurt and defiance she poured into them replays on a loop. It's maddening. I feel like I'm being pulled in a million directions, torn between what I know and what I feel, between logic and emotion.

A part of me yearns to chase after her, to pull her into a tight embrace and apologize for letting things spiral out of control. As the desire rises, so does my pride. Why should I be the one to mend fences? She was the one who crossed the line, who let emotions seep into our arrangement. She was the one who challenged the parameters we painstakingly set to avoid this problem.

I adjust the rearview mirror, catching a fleeting glimpse of Megan's figure, smaller now in the distance. My heart clenches. Was it really just about boundaries and lines? Or have I, too, been fooling myself? Was it possible that I had started to feel something deeper than our mere pretense?

As I pull out of the parking lot, the cool night air filtering in through the slightly opened window brings with it memories of our shared moments. The times she laughed at my jokes, her eyes sparkling with mirth; the times she reached out to me, bridging the gap between pretense and reality. I remember the soft touch of her hand, the lingering scent of her perfume, the sound of her voice whispering in my ear.

With those memories also comes the sharp reminder of why I needed her in the first place. My father's expectations, the looming threat of losing my inheritance. The need to present a united front, a perfect couple, to the world. It's all about survival, about securing a future. Emotions are a very dangerous detour that could derail our whole facade.

Shaking my head, I try to clear away the fog of confusion. My thoughts drift to our argument. The intensity of it, the raw emotions laid bare. I had snapped, allowing my pride to win out over my better judgment. And yet, wasn't she equally to blame? Had she not used the emotions card to provoke me? She knew just how to push my buttons.

The internal debate continues as I drive, my thoughts oscillating between guilt and indignation. The city lights whizz by, but I barely notice. My mind is lost in the labyrinth of thoughts and emotions, trying to make sense of the tangled web we've woven between our lives.

After what seems like hours, I finally pull up to my apartment building. The dimly lit lobby provides a stark contrast to the maelstrom of feelings whirling inside me. As I step out of the car, I glance up at the night sky, searching for answers among the stars.

They remain silent, leaving me with nothing but questions. Questions that, deep down, I fear I already know the answers to.

Chapter Twelve

Megan

Stepping into my office, the cool air surrounds me, a welcome relief from the city's heat. Bright sunlight filters through the windows, illuminating the plush chairs and sleek desk. On it, lay stacks of paperwork—contracts, invoices, and assorted files—a testament to the bustling wedding planning business I've built.

Miss Barker and Mr. Davis are already waiting, engrossed in conversation, their laughter tinkling through the room. I force a smile, trying to shake off the remnants of last night's argument with Carter. I need to focus on the job at hand.

"Good morning," I greet, extending my hand to each.

"Morning, Miss Medina," Mr. Davis responds, his smile genuine. Miss Barker simply nods, her attention seemingly diverted by a picture of a centerpiece on my desk.

We dive straight into the details. I've pulled up multiple options for them based on our last discussion. As we talk about the venue, the décor, the ambiance they're hoping to achieve, I can see their excitement. It's infectious and momentarily distracts me from the turmoil in my personal life.

"So, have you finalized the caterers yet?" I ask, turning my attention to one of the more crucial elements of any wedding.

Mr. Davis nods. "Yes, we went with La Cuisine Fantastique. Their tasting session was divine."

"That's wonderful," I say, making a note. "I'll just call them to discuss the final menu and dates."

Dialing the caterer's number, I am greeted with a cheerful voice on the other end. "La Cuisine Fantastique, this is Maria speaking. How can I help you?"

"Hi Maria, it's Megan. I'm calling about the Barker-Davis wedding. We're looking to finalize the menu and dates."

There's a pause, long enough to raise concern. "Oh, I'm sorry, Miss Megan. Didn't someone call to cancel that booking yesterday?"

My heart sinks, confusion and frustration bubbling up. "Cancel? No, there must be a mistake."

Maria sounds genuinely apologetic. "It was a man who called. He confirmed the wedding details and then requested a cancellation."

I shoot a perplexed look at Mr. Davis. "Did you call to cancel?"

He looks just as surprised. "Absolutely not! Why would I cancel when everything was coming together so perfectly?"

Miss Barker's fingers drum impatiently on the table. "So, someone just impersonated us and canceled our booking?"

"I'm so sorry for the inconvenience," Maria interjects. "Miss Megan, we'll do everything we can to sort this out."

I nod, though she can't see it. "Thank you, Maria. We'll get back to you soon. Do you know who called?"

"The man said his name was Davis." I can hear the embarrassment in her voice. "Clearly, he wasn't who he said he was. I am *so* sorry."

I wince. "It's not your fault, but please have this sorted as soon as possible. Thanks."

Hanging up, I take a deep breath, trying to hold back the frustration threatening to spill over. Who would do this, and why?

Miss Barker looks worried. "Miss Medina, do you think it's someone trying to sabotage our wedding?"

Mr. Davis shakes his head. "It doesn't make any sense."

The wheels in my head start turning. Could it have something to do with the whole charade with Carter? Or is this just an unfortunate mix-up?

Determined to steer the conversation away from the disappointing news about the caterer, I glance at my notes and take a deep breath, forcing a smile. "Alright, let's move on to the next item. Have you decided on a photographer yet?"

Miss Barker's eyes brighten. "Oh, yes! We found this amazing independent local photographer, Barbara Weintz. Her portfolio is breathtaking."

Mr. Davis nods enthusiastically. "We had a chat with her and immediately felt a connection. She understands the vibe we're going for, and her candid shots are just mesmerizing."

"That's great to hear," I respond, scribbling down the name. "Having a photographer who truly understands your vision can make all the difference. I'll give her a call right now and confirm the details."

I quickly dial Barbara's number, hoping this conversation goes better than the last one. After a few rings, a bubbly voice greets me, "Hello, Barbara Weintz speaking."

"Hi Barbara, this is Megan Medina. I'm working with Whitney Barker and Landon Davis for their wedding. They mentioned they've booked you for their big day, and I just wanted to discuss some of the specifics."

Another pause. Another sinking feeling.

"I'm so sorry, Megan, but Mr. Davis called me on Wednesday to cancel the booking," Barbara says, confusion evident in her tone.

My heart drops, and I glance over at Mr. Davis, who has turned a shade paler. "Mr. Davis, did you call Barbara to cancel?"

He looks as stunned as I feel. "No, I swear I didn't. Why on earth would I do that?"

Miss Barker's anxiety is palpable as she interjects, "Miss Medina, this can't be a coincidence. First the caterer, now the photographer. Someone is deliberately trying to sabotage our wedding!"

"I'm truly sorry about this mix-up, Megan," Barbara says on the other end. "I don't know what's happening, but if you need me, I'll make sure to be there for the wedding. My commitment to my clients is unwavering."

I sigh, defeated. "Thank you, Barbara. I appreciate that. We'll be in touch soon."

Ending the call, I take a moment to gather my thoughts, trying to think of a way to salvage the situation.

Mr. Davis runs a hand through his hair, clearly stressed. "Why is someone doing this to us?"

"I don't know," I admit, feeling the responsibility weighing heavily on my shoulders. "I promise you, I'll get to the bottom of this. We'll make sure everything is in order for your big day."

Miss Barker takes a deep breath, clearly trying to hold back tears. "Thank you, Miss Medina. We trust you."

I nod, a renewed sense of determination filling me. "Thank you for understanding. I'll personally handle everything from now on and ensure there are no further mix-ups."

While the couple nods, their trust in me evident, I can't shake the nagging feeling that something bigger is at play here.

Someone is going to great lengths to sabotage this wedding, and I'm determined to find out who.

After reassuring my clients, I can't ignore the rising tide of anxiety within me. My intuition screams that something is amiss. I decide to reach out to all the vendors we've engaged so far. The more I find out, the more the pieces of this peculiar puzzle begin to click together.

First, the florist. She confirms that the order is intact, no cancellations there. A sigh of relief. However, the baker responsible for the cake tells a different story. "Got a call yesterday, saying it was off," she says in a bewildered voice. "They said they'd found another place. Had no idea it wasn't genuine."

By the time I've reached the end of the list, half of our bookings are apparently canceled. My frustration grows, but I push it down, focusing on gathering all the information I can. "Could you describe the voice of the man who called to cancel?" I ask the DJ, hoping to pick out some consistency.

There's a thoughtful pause on the other end of the line. "Sounded mid-thirties, I'd say. Had a distinct Boston accent. He was a bit awkward, like he wasn't sure of what he was saying. Honestly, I thought it was a little weird at the time."

A Boston accent. Awkward. My mind instantly jumps to a face: Tim Donnelly.

It makes a chilling kind of sense. Tim's behavior at the Fitzgerald Hotel had been off. Now, with the description matching him almost too perfectly, my suspicions flare into near certainty. The question now is, *why*.

I think back to a few weeks ago, when I left my laptop in my usual meeting room to go to reception... could Tim have figured out my password and decided to snoop?

"Why would Tim sabotage my clients?" I muse aloud, my thoughts are frenzied. Instead of confronting Tim immediately, I first think to inform Carter. We need to be united against whatever is happening, regardless of our recent disagreement. I pull out my phone, dialing Carter's number, but after a few rings, it diverts to voicemail. With a sigh, I hang up and decide to send a text.

Carter, we have a problem. Call me ASAP.

Seconds turn to minutes, but no response comes. My patience is wearing thin. Determined to get answers, I drive to The Vivante Grand. The gold and marble foyer welcomes me, as it always does, but this time the grandeur does little to elevate my mood.

"Hello, Megan," greets Laura, the receptionist, with a friendly smile. "How can I help you today?"

"I'm looking for Tim Donnelly. Is he around?" I ask.

Laura's smile falters slightly. "I'm afraid Tim isn't working today. Is there something I can help you with?"

Frustration bubbles up within me, but I try to keep it in check. "No, it's fine. I'll catch him later."

As I turn to leave, two maids walk by, deeply engrossed in their conversation. I wouldn't have paid them any mind, but a snippet of their chatter catches my attention.

"Did you hear about Mr. Wright?" one of them says in a hushed tone, but loud enough for me to hear.

Her co-worker, a younger woman, looks around and whispers, "You mean about him and that Megan girl?"

I freeze in place, doing my best to blend in and not alert them to my presence.

The first maid nods eagerly. "Yeah, I heard they're not even really engaged. It's just a cover-up."

"What for?"

"Apparently, he's got another woman in San Francisco. Someone he's been seeing secretly for months. The word is, Megan is just a ploy to divert attention."

The younger maid's eyes widen. "No way! Mr. Wright would never!"

The first maid smirks. "You'd be surprised what people with money do. There's even a rumor that he's involved in some shady business deals on the side. I overheard it from the bartender. He said he heard it from someone at that fancy restaurant across the street."

Shady business deals. A secret lover in San Francisco. My heart sinks. These rumors, if they gain traction, could be incredibly damaging to Carter's reputation, not to mention the appearance of the authenticity of our charade.

"I always knew there was something off about him," the younger maid comments, shaking her head.

The two continue their conversation, moving farther away from me, their words fade into indistinct murmurs.

Once they're out of earshot, I pull myself together. This new gossip hits me hard, but I need to remain focused. First, there's the issue with Tim possibly sabotaging my clients. Now, there's the growing web of rumors about Carter.

I need answers, fast.

I glance down at my phone, noting the little check mark beside my message to Carter. It's been marked as read, but there's still no response. A mix of annoyance and hurt bubbles within me. Is he intentionally avoiding me after our spat? I exhale heavily, my breath forming a visible cloud in the cool air of the lobby.

On one hand, his silence stings. Regardless of our personal feelings, we're in the middle of a situation that could potentially harm both our reputations, not to mention my client's plans.

We need to be in sync, working together. His lack of response feels like a betrayal.

On the other hand, the raw emotion from our argument still lingers in the forefront of my mind. The harsh words, the accusatory tones—it's all too fresh. Perhaps it's better he hasn't responded. In my current state, I'm not sure if our conversation would be productive or just another explosive altercation.

Laura's voice interrupts my internal debate. "Is everything okay, Megan?"

I force a tight smile. "Yes, thank you, Laura. Just a minor hiccup. I'll handle it."

She nods, giving me a sympathetic look. "If you need anything, let me know."

I appreciate the sentiment, but right now, what I need most is clarity—and distance from Carter. "Thanks, Laura. Take care."

Exiting the entrance of The Vivante Grand, the hot air hits my face mirroring the stifling emotions inside me. The parking lot is dotted with cars, glistening under the afternoon sun. A family with two young kids hurries by, the children's laughter echoing, reminding me that life goes on regardless of my personal drama.

Walking toward my car, I pull out my keys. The sounds of a distant conversation distract me. Turning my head, I see a couple arguing near a sleek black sedan. The woman is crying, mascara running down her face, while the man looks desperate, his hands gesturing animatedly.

Witnessing this raw display of emotions brings back a rush of memories from the night before, of my own tearful face and Carter's conflicted expression. Even amidst the concrete and cars, human emotions have a way of cutting through, exposing vulnerabilities and truths.

I unlock my car and slide into the driver's seat, placing my purse beside me. As I start the engine, I take one last glance at my phone, half-expecting a response from Carter. But the screen remains blank, save for the time and date.

Maybe he's still processing our argument, or maybe he's caught up in the chaos of these damaging rumors. Either way, I feel a pang of regret. I allowed my feelings to cloud my judgment, and now we're more estranged than ever.

Backing out of my parking spot, I decide to head to my apartment. I need some time to think, to strategize. Whatever is going on—with Tim, the rumors, and my relationship with Carter—I need to get to the bottom of it.

Chapter Thirteen

Carter

The sprawling windows of my office reveal the dazzling L.A. cityscape of towering edifices. It's a view I've always taken pride in, but right now, every shimmering light outside seems dim in comparison to the tension that fills this room.

Megan sits across from me, her expression hard to read. Taking a deep breath, I lean in, finding my voice. "Megan," I begin, trying to sound firm, yet also revealing a bit of vulnerability, "I've thought about it, and even after everything, our disagreements and the heated words, I still think we should press on with the ruse of this engagement."

Her eyes search mine. There's a flicker there, a momentary glint of... surprise. Hope? I can't quite pinpoint it. "I was immature for not responding to your messages," I admit. "My emotions got the best of me."

She looks as if she's expecting more. An outright apology. Old habits die hard, and the full weight of my pride is still holding me back from going all in.

"There's more," I say, pushing on. "I believe we should move ahead and plan our own wedding. It's the next logical step in this plan of ours."

She looks stunned and I watch her closely, gauging her reaction. As she processes my words, I can see her mental gears turning, likely recalling the troubling rumors that have been circulating.

"Carter," she says, the hesitation clear in her voice. "With the rumors and everything... Do you really think this is the right move now? They're not just affecting us, but they're also impacting my clients and my reputation."

I nod, absorbing her words. "I get where you're coming from," I concede. "Pushing forward, showing the world our commitment—couldn't that be the answer to combat these baseless rumors?"

She seems to be in deep thought, contemplating. "It's not as simple as that," she finally replies. "These rumors, they're vicious. Part of me thinks that moving forward might silence them, but another part fears it might only make things worse."

The room becomes heavy with silence, a contemplative stillness as we each wrestle with our thoughts.

I finally break it. "Megan, all I want is for this to work. For both of us."

She meets my gaze, those deep eyes revealing a myriad of emotions. "I want that too," she murmurs. "We have to be smart, though. We need a solid plan."

I nod, feeling a shudder of relief. I'm left wondering about our future, about the path we've chosen, and where it will eventually lead us.

"There's something you should know, though."

Just like that, the moment shatters.

"Tim Donnelly has been snooping around. I don't know if anything will come of it, but he's suspicious. Of us."

Megan's revelation catches me off guard. "Tim Donnelly? I always knew him to be ambitious, even competitive, but sabotage? Why would he go to such lengths?" I ask, trying to process the information.

She shrugs, looking exasperated. "Like I said, it might be jealousy. He's had this strange infatuation with me since I first started working at the Grand. When he saw us together, his whole demeanor changed. Or perhaps he knows about our agreement and wants to expose us, tarnish both our reputations."

I clench my fists involuntarily, feeling the anger rise in me. How dare he? If Tim's trying to play games with us, he's picked the wrong opponent. "He's messing with the wrong people," I hiss, glaring into the distance. "If he is behind this, I swear I'll make sure he never works in this industry again."

Megan looks alarmed, reaching out to touch my arm gently. "Carter, I understand you're angry. I am too; but please think rationally. We need to handle this with care. Going headfirst into it could backfire, or even make things worse."

Her words barely register in my mind. My heart is racing, filled with a strange mixture of fury and protectiveness. I don't like being played, and I especially don't appreciate someone targeting Megan.

I grab my coat, throwing it over my arm. "I need to sort this out. If Tim is behind it, he's going to wish he never crossed our path."

"Carter!" Megan's voice is urgent, her eyes wide with concern. "Please, think this through. Do you really want to confront him now, in this state?"

I pause for a moment, glancing back at her. For a second, the world seems to slow down. The way she looks at me, the worry clear in her eyes—it's almost endearing. This isn't just about me anymore. It's about us, our plan, our reputations.

"Yes," I say with determination. "We can't let him, or anyone else, get away with this. We need to protect what we've built."

She stands up, looking like she's ready to argue, but then she lets out a long sigh. "Alright but promise me you'll be careful. We don't know for certain if Tim is behind all this. Even if he is, we need evidence. You know how the industry talks. We don't want to be the villains here."

Her words make sense. As much as I want to march straight into Tim's office and demand answers, I recognize that caution is needed. "Okay," I say, taking a deep breath. "I'm not going to sit around and let this continue. We'll gather evidence, but if it points to him, I will make him pay."

Megan nods, her expression serious. "Agreed. Just... be careful."

As I watch her walk out of the office, I'm not only armed with a determination to uncover the truth but also with the knowledge that Megan genuinely cares about our partnership. Maybe, just maybe, she cares about me too.

Back in my office an hour later, the skyline outside now dark, I'm lost in thought when there's a knock on my door. Margot appears, her usual composure replaced by a look of concern.

"Carter," she begins, hesitating slightly, "I need to tell you something. Josh Warrington came by earlier. He was demanding a meeting with you."

I straighten up, my attention fully on her. "Warrington was here? What did he want?"

Margot fidgets, clearly uneasy. "I'm not sure, but he seemed... angry. I told him you were unavailable, and he left in a huff. I'm worried he might cause trouble."

Josh Warrington's name alone is enough to make me wary. He's been a nuisance for years, a constant thought in the back of my mind. The competition in my line of business has always been harsh, but there's nobody else quite like *Josh*. Our expansions have been faster and more successful than his and he refuses to believe it's Vivante's team pulling this off. His pettiness knows no bounds. And is way out of proportion.

Which brings me to ask, "Did he say why he wanted to meet?" I ask, trying to piece together his unexpected visit with the ongoing drama surrounding Megan and me.

"He didn't specify, but I overheard him mumbling something about your wedding with Megan as he was leaving. It sounded... sarcastic."

My heart sinks. If Josh has gotten wind of the rumors surrounding Megan and me, or worse, if he suspects our engagement is a facade, this could complicate matters significantly. Josh's the type to use any leverage he can get his hands on.

I drum my fingers on the desk, thinking. "Did he leave any message?"

"Just that he'd be 'in touch'," Margot replies.

I nod, my mind racing. "Thanks, Margot. If he contacts you again, let me know immediately."

She nods and leaves, closing the door behind her. I lean back in my chair, gazing out at the city lights. Josh's sudden interest in my personal life is troubling. If he knows about Megan and me, I'm sure he wouldn't hesitate to use it to fuel the fire.

I pick up my phone, contemplating warning Megan. After our earlier confrontation, I hesitate. Instead, I decide to gather more information before involving her further. If Josh's sniffing around, I need to be prepared.

First, I need to tighten up our story, ensure there are no cracks for Josh or anyone else to exploit. Then, I need to have a conversation with Tim Donnelly. If he's indeed the source of the rumors and cancellations, he could be the weak link that Josh is using against us. Megan said she ran into Tim at the Fitzgerald so it's possible he's working with Josh to undermine me.

Picking up the phone, I dial the Vivante Grand's number. My fingers tap impatiently on the desk as I wait for the call to connect. The familiar receptionist's voice greets me, and I cut straight to the chase.

"I need to speak with Tim Donnelly, now," I demand, trying to keep my tone even.

There's a brief pause, then a click, and Tim's voice comes through, tinged with surprise and a hint of excitement. "Mr. Wright! To what do I owe this pleasure? I never expected a personal call from you."

"Cut the pleasantries, Tim," I snap, my patience wearing thin. "I'm calling about something serious. There have been some... irregularities with the Barker-Davis wedding. Cancellations that were supposedly made by them but weren't."

Tim's tone shifts, a note of confusion in his voice. "Irregularities? I'm not sure I follow, sir."

I lean forward, my voice hardening. "Let's not play games, now. You're the head of the events management team at the Vivante, aren't you? I have reason to believe you're behind the cancellations."

There's a pause on the other end, and when Tim speaks again, his voice is laced with feigned shock. "Mr. Wright, I assure you

I have nothing to do with this. Why would I harm the hotel's business?"

I grit my teeth, frustration mounting. "Because you've taken an unhealthy interest in Megan. Now, suddenly, her clients are facing anonymous cancellations. It's more than a coincidence."

"Sir, I admit I have a high regard for Miss Medina, but I would never jeopardize my career or the hotel's reputation over personal feelings," Tim replies, his tone a mix of earnestness and indignation.

I take a deep breath, trying to keep my anger in check. "Listen, Tim. If I find out you're lying, there will be severe consequences."

Tim's voice is steady, infuriatingly calm. "I understand, Mr. Wright, and I respect that; but I'm telling you, you're barking up the wrong tree here. I have no part in this."

The conversation goes around in circles, with Tim maintaining his innocence and me getting nowhere. Frustrated and with no new information, I finally end the call. I sit back, rubbing my temples, feeling a headache brewing.

If Tim is telling the truth, then who's behind the sabotage? If he's lying, how do I prove it? The situation feels more tangled than ever, and my direct accusations might have just escalated things. Megan was right, I shouldn't have contacted Tim without more proof.

I glance at the clock on the wall, its hands inching toward eight o'clock. The office is quiet, the usual hustle of the day long since subsided. I feel the weight of exhaustion pressing down on me, but my mind is still racing with the mounting problems at hand. The workload, the issues with Megan and our relationship, Tim's potential sabotage, and now Josh Warrington's unexpected involvement. It feels unending.

Picking up the phone, I dial Margot, who answers after the first ring.

"I'm calling it a night. You should, too."

"Alright, Mr. Wright. Anything you need me to handle before I leave?" Her voice is steady, always ready to assist.

I rub the bridge of my nose, thinking. "Can you follow up with legal first thing in the morning? Check our options regarding the rumors and any potential action we might take."

"Of course, sir. If Mr. Warrington tries to contact you again?"

"Let me know immediately. Margot," I pause, a weary sigh escaping me, "Thank you."

"Of course, Mr. Wright. Have a good night."

I hang up and gather my things. The walk to the parking lot is a quiet one. The usually bustling corridors of the office building are now deserted, the only sound is my footsteps echoing off the walls.

As I reach my car, I can't help but let my thoughts drift back to Tim and Josh. If Tim is behind the sabotage, how far is he willing to go? Josh Warrington, with his sudden interest in my personal affairs, only complicates matters further. His reputation in the business world is notorious, and if he suspects our engagement is a facade, he could use it against us.

I slide into the driver's seat, the familiar scent of leather enveloping me. As I start the engine, I realize that no matter how much I want to separate my personal life from my business, it's all intertwined now. Between Megan, Tim, and Josh—they're all pieces of a complex puzzle that I need to solve.

Driving out of the parking lot, the city lights blur into streaks as I speed down the street. My mind is a whirlwind of strategies and contingencies. One thing is clear—I need to make sure I'm one step ahead of any future problems that could arise.

As the city skyline fades behind me, I'm reminded that in this world of high stakes and power plays, it's not just about surviving; it's about staying in control. I intend to do just that.

Chapter Fourteen

Megan

Bright sunlight pours through my office window. I'm feeling restless this morning, unsettled by everything that's been happening. After a sleepless night spent tossing and turning, I decide to try calling Carter again. But like yesterday, there's no answer, his phone is ringing straight to voicemail.

Is he avoiding me, or is he simply swamped with work? The uncertainty gnaws at me. On impulse, I decide to go to his office. Maybe a face-to-face conversation will clear the air, help us figure out how to handle the Tim situation.

Arriving at his office building, the secretary at the front desk greets me with a polite smile. "Good morning, Miss Medina. Mr. Wright is in today. Would you like me to announce you?"

I shake my head. "No, thank you. I'll surprise him."

She nods, understanding the delicate dance of personal and professional boundaries we're playing. I take the elevator up to his top-floor office, rehearsing in my mind what I want to say to him.

As I step out into the hallway, I nearly collide with Carter, who's just stepping out of his office, dressed impeccably in a sharp suit. He's clearly on his way out, and the surprise on his face is clear.

"Megan," he says, a little taken aback. "What brings you here?"

"I tried calling," I start, feeling slightly defensive. "We need to talk."

He checks his watch, his expression torn. "I have a meeting," he begins, but I cut him off.

"Cancel it," I suggest, trying to sound more confident than I feel. "Have lunch with me instead. It'll make us look good," I add quickly, though secretly, I just want to spend time with him, clear the air.

He hesitates for a moment, then nods. "Alright. Let's do it."

We head toward the elevator. The silence that falls between us is thick with unspoken words and lingering tension. I glance at him, trying to gauge his thoughts, but his expression is unreadable.

We wait for the elevator together, standing in silence as the numbers tick by. Twelfth floor, thirteenth, top floor... then it dings and we step in. It's only us.

The elevator hums as it descends, the numbers on the panel counting down the floors. Just as I'm about to attempt some small talk, the elevator shudders violently, causing us both to grab onto the handrails. Then, with a jarring halt, it stops on the tenth floor.

Carter immediately starts pressing buttons, but the elevator remains stubbornly immobile. His jaw clenches in clear frustration. He hits the emergency button, but still, there's no response.

"Great," I mutter, reaching for my phone to call for help, only to realize it's not there. "I must've left my phone in the car."

Carter's frustration is palpable as he leans against the wall of the elevator. "This is just what we needed," he says dryly.

I try to lighten the mood. "Well, someone's bound to notice eventually. Especially if their CEO is missing from an important meeting."

He doesn't seem to appreciate the attempt at humor. Instead, he just rubs his temples, clearly trying to calm himself.

Seeing no other option, I slide down against the elevator wall, settling onto the floor. "Might as well get comfortable," I suggest. "Could be a while."

After a moment, he reluctantly joins me on the floor, his back against the opposite wall. The close confines of the elevator make the situation feel more intimate, more personal.

I glance over at him, and despite the frustration of the situation, I feel a strange sense of camaraderie. Here we are, stuck in an elevator, forced to confront not just the physical proximity but the complexities of our arrangement.

"So," I start, breaking the silence, "about Tim and our wedding plans... I assume you've been making the arrangements?"

Carter sighs, his gaze meeting mine. "You're the wedding planner, not me, but I figured we should have it at the Grand..." He trails off, shaking his head.

I sigh, trying to ignore the flutter of discomfort in my stomach. "It's just hard to believe we're going ahead with it," I say, more to myself than him.

The temperature in the elevator begins to drop, the cold seeping into my bones. I wrap my arms around myself, trying to conserve warmth. Carter notices and, without a word, takes off his coat and hands it to me.

"Here, you'll freeze in that blouse," he says, his tone gentle.

I hesitate for a moment, then accept the coat, draping it over my shoulders. It's warm, carrying his scent—a subtle mix of cologne and something distinctly Carter.

I find myself surprised by this gesture, this small act of thoughtfulness from a man who often hides behind a facade of strict professionalism and detachment. It's these moments, these glimpses of the real Carter, that confuse me, blurring the lines of our arrangement.

"Thank you," I murmur, pulling the coat tighter around me. There's a softness in his eyes that I haven't seen before, and it tugs at something inside me.

We sit in silence for a moment before Carter speaks up, his voice softer now, almost reflective. "I didn't really care about that meeting," he admits, staring at the elevator doors as if they hold the answers to his inner turmoil. "Most of these meetings are just a waste of time."

I turn to face him, intrigued. "Then why do it? Why spend so much time on something you don't care about?"

He lets out a weary sigh. "It's all part of the job, Megan. I didn't even want to be CEO, not initially. My father, when he first fell ill years ago, convinced me it was the right thing to do. He said I had a knack for business, that I could take our company to new heights."

I nod, understanding dawning on me. "It's not what you wanted?"

Carter shakes his head, a bitter smile playing on his lips. "I wanted to travel, see the world. Maybe even live abroad for a few years. Then... duty called."

The vulnerability in his admission catches me off guard. It's easy to forget that behind the title and the responsibilities, there's a person with dreams and doubts.

"Now?" I ask gently.

"Now, I'm... I'm not enough." The words come out bitterly. "I'll never live up to my father's legacy." His voice is barely above a whisper, filled with a raw honesty that makes my heart ache for him.

In that moment, the barriers between us seem to crumble. I see Carter not as the CEO, not as my fake fiancé, but as a man burdened by expectations and unfulfilled desires. It's a revelation that shifts something within me.

Wrapped in Carter's coat, the warmth seeping into me, I'm starting to see him in a whole new light. The man I've known as confident and controlled is now revealing a vulnerability that I never knew existed. It's in these unguarded moments that I find my attraction to him increasing, not for the man he pretends to be, but for the man he actually is.

Feeling a sudden surge of boldness, perhaps fueled by our shared confinement and the raw honesty of the moment, I decide to open up too. "I know what you mean about feeling like you're not enough," I start, my voice softer than I intend. "I've never been married, barely had a serious relationship. Most of my family have settled down, and here I am, planning weddings for others."

I pause, looking down at my hands. "I love my freedom, the thrill of running my own business. Sometimes, the weight of other people's expectations is hard to shake off."

"I thought I'd get married once, but after Brady..."

"Brady?"

"My ex." Talking about it now makes me shiver. "He was... he wasn't a good person. I had to call the police once. After we broke up, he started stalking me."

Carter turns his full attention to me, his eyes softening. "That's awful, you don't deserve shit like that," he says, moving a fraction closer.

The air between us feels charged, each breath heavy with unspoken emotion. His proximity, the intensity of his gaze, sends a thrill through me, awakening feelings I've been trying to suppress.

"Yeah, well, my mother still thinks I should settle down. Apparently, one bad experience isn't an excuse to stay single."

He reaches out, his hand tentatively resting on mine. "You don't have to be what others expect, Megan. You're incredible just the way you are... even if you drive me mad."

His words resonate deep within me, echoing my own thoughts and fears. For a moment, I allow myself to just be, to appreciate the connection growing between us.

Then, slowly, almost hesitantly, Carter leans in. The space between us diminishes until I can feel his breath mingling with mine. My heart races, anticipation building. Then, his lips are on mine, soft and questioning at first, but growing more confident as I respond in kind.

The kiss is a revelation, a mixture of tenderness and passion that makes my heart pound. All the tension, the uncertainty, melts away, leaving only the sensation of his lips against mine, the warmth of his body so close to me.

As we pull away, there's a moment of silence. Carter looks at me, his eyes reflecting a mix of thoughts and questions.

All I see is the man I've grown to care for, not just as a partner in a business arrangement, but as someone I genuinely want in my life.

In the aftermath of the kiss, desire courses through me. The warmth of his lips still lingers on mine, sparking a yearning I hadn't fully acknowledged until now. Without thinking, I lean forward and capture his lips again, this time with more urgency, more force.

Carter responds immediately, his hands moving to my waist, pressing me gently against the elevator wall. The confined space amplifies every touch, every breath. He straddles my hips, his body aligning perfectly with mine. The heat between us builds, a tangible, electric current that makes my heart race and my body ache for more.

I slide my hands up his chest, feeling the solid muscle beneath his shirt. His heart pounds against my palms, matching the rhythm of my own. He kisses me deeply, passionately, each movement deliberate, as if he's trying to communicate everything he can't admit out loud.

Our breaths mingle, quick and ragged, as the kiss deepens. The teasing touch of his lips, the gentle nipping of my lip sends shivers down my spine, the way his fingers trail along my jawline—it's all overwhelming, intoxicating.

I find myself responding with equal urgency, my fingers tangling in his hair, pulling him closer. There's a playful challenge in my movements, a silent invitation for him to explore further. His hand drifts downward, tracing the curve of my waist, and over my hip, coming to rest on my ass and giving it a playful squeeze, sending sparks of desire coursing through me.

Our kisses become messy, desperate, as his erection presses against the inside of my thigh. Every touch is a tease, a promise of what could be, of what we both want but aren't sure we should pursue. It's a dangerous game, one that threatens to make our agreement even more ambiguous.

As we pull away, breathless and flushed, the reality of our situation slowly sinks back in. We're still in an elevator, stuck between floors.

I look into Carter's eyes, seeing a reflection of my own thoughts—surprise, desire, and a hint of uncertainty shows in those flushed cheeks and wide eyes.

"Wow," I whisper, the word barely audible.

Carter nods, a wry smile on his lips. "Yeah... "

Chapter Fifteen

Carter

I stare at her for a long moment, admiring the way her hair brushes against her slender shoulders; how her flush of her cheeks contrasts with her tanned skin so well, making her even more beautiful.

I'm still half-hard, eager for more, but I never get the chance—the elevator unexpectedly dings back to life, Megan startles beside me, breaking the spell that had enveloped us.

We hastily separate, both standing and trying to regain our composure. My mind is still reeling from the intensity of our interaction, the passion that had so unexpectedly flared between us.

I avoid discussing what just happened, unsure of how to navigate this uncharted territory. However, I find myself standing a little closer to Megan than necessary as the elevator descends. The air between us is thick with unspoken words and the echo of our shared desire.

Megan stands beside me, still wrapped in my coat, the warmth of her intoxicating.

Reaching the ground floor, the doors slide open, revealing the busy lobby of my office building. We step out together into the hustle and bustle of the outside world, a stark contrast to the isolated intimacy we shared in the elevator.

As we approach the main entrance, Margot rushes up to me, a look of concern on her face. "Mr. Wright, I've been trying to reach you," she says, slightly out of breath. "Your brother left a message. He's been trying to call you."

I frown, a sense of foreboding settling over me. "What did he say?"

She hesitates, her eyes flicking to Megan before returning to mine. "It's your father. He's been re-admitted to the hospital, although he didn't give much detail. I've called your driver."

The news hits me like a physical blow. My father, discharged only 2 days ago, is back in the hospital. My hands shake as I try to recover, my mind already racing with thoughts of everything that still needs to be done. "Thank you, Margot. I'll handle it."

Turning to Megan, I see the concern etched on her face. "I have to go," I say, the words feeling inadequate.

She nods, her expression sympathetic. "Of course. Do you want me to come with you?"

He pauses. "No, not today. I don't want this to be how you meet him."

"All right. Let me know if there's anything I can do."

I offer her a tight smile, appreciating her offer. "Thank you, Megan. I'll...I'll call you."

As I stride toward the car, the earlier passion and confusion are momentarily pushed aside, replaced by the singular focus of my father's health. We all knew that he was sick, but the reality had never settled in before. Until now.

On the ride to the hospital, my mind is in turmoil. Leaving Megan so abruptly after what transpired between us feels wrong, but family duty calls. The familiar streets pass by in a haze, my thoughts consumed by my father's condition and the memories of our complex relationship.

Upon arriving at the hospital, I rush through the sliding doors and head straight to the reception desk.

"I need to see my father," I tell the receptionist, trying to keep my voice steady. "He's been admitted. Bradford Wright is the name."

The receptionist types into her computer, then looks up. "He's been admitted for pneumonia," she informs me, her tone professional yet empathetic.

Pneumonia. The word sends a chill down my spine. In most cases, it wouldn't be cause for extreme concern, but my father's immune system is already compromised. It's serious.

"Which ward?" I ask, my urgency growing.

"Intensive care."

She gives me the details, and I stride toward the elevators, my heart pounding in my chest.

Reaching the ward, I see my brother, Colton, waiting outside a private room. He looks up as I approach, his brows furrowed. He looks exhausted, his dark hair a mess and his five o'clock shadow making him look haggard.

"Colton," I greet him, the familial tensions between us momentarily set aside.

"Carter," he responds, his voice tired. "He's in there. They're saying it's serious, he's on oxygen."

I nod, swallowing the lump in my throat. Despite our differences, the concern for our father unites us in this moment. "Have you been in to see him?"

Colton shakes his head. "They were limiting visitors until they got him stabilized. I was about to go in when you arrived."

We stand there in silence, the weight of the situation hanging heavily between us. The man who had been a towering figure in our lives, commanding our paths and decisions, now laying weak and vulnerable just a few feet away.

After a few moments, a nurse exits the room, her expression somber. "You can see him now, but please, keep it brief. He needs to rest."

Colton gestures for me to go first. I hesitate, a scowl forming. I haven't been to see him in person since he dropped the bombshell ultimatum regarding my inheritance.

Taking a deep breath, I step into the room. The sight of my father, lying so still and frail, is a stark contrast to the robust, commanding figure I've always known. He's hooked up to oxygen and a drip, the tubes stark against his skin.

"Dad," I whisper, approaching his bedside.

His eyes flutter open, a glimmer of recognition in them as he sees me. "Carter," he murmurs, his voice weak.

Colton and I each take a seat in chairs on opposite sides of the bed. Colton reaches out to take Dad's hand and squeezes gently.

He looks at me, clearly expecting me to offer words of comfort but I come up dry. There's nothing to say that can help, and nothing I *want* to say anyway.

The rhythmic beeping of the heart monitor serves as the only sound in the otherwise silent room until Colton breaks the quiet with a biting remark.

"It's almost comical, you know. How suddenly you're the dutiful son, now that there's talk of Dad's inheritance," he says, his voice dripping with sarcasm.

His words strike a nerve, and my temper, already frayed from the events of the day, flares up. "That's not fair, Colton. You know the relationship Dad and I had was anything but simple."

Colton lets out a bitter laugh. "Simple? It *is* simple, Carter. You were the golden boy, the expected heir, while I was nothing more than an afterthought. Now, here you are, acting like you've been here all along."

I feel a rush of anger, my voice rising despite my efforts to control it. "You think I wanted any of this? Dad made these decisions, not me. I never asked to be put in this position."

"Oh, but you never refused it either, did you?" Colton shoots back, his voice growing louder. "This past year, while you were off attending to business, I was here, dealing with family matters, taking care of Dad. Where were you?"

His accusation hits close to home, stirring up a mix of guilt and resentment. "I was doing what I thought was best for the family, for the business," I counter. "It wasn't just handed to me. I worked for it."

"Worked for it?" Colton's face contorts with anger. "You were handed everything on a silver platter. Now, you suddenly show up to claim your prize. Don't think I haven't figured out why you're marrying that Megan girl. Dad says he'll give you the inheritance if you settle down, and now suddenly you're engaged."

His sudden bitterness takes me aback. I knew Colton harbored resentment, but I hadn't realized just how deep it ran.

"Inheritance or no," I say through gritted teeth. "Dad's ill. *Really* ill. Does it matter why I'm here, so long as I am?"

"If you care," He scoffs. "You have a funny way of showing it. You were never here when it mattered. You haven't cared about Dad the way I have."

His words sting, but they also awaken a conflicting emotion within me. A part of me has always envied Colton's relationship with our father, their ability to connect on a level I never could, despite his absences and travels. And then his rebellion, his decision to manage movie theatres, avoiding anything to do with the hotel industry.

"You're right, Colt," I concede, my anger giving way to a reluctant admission. "I wasn't here as much as I should have been, but that doesn't mean I didn't care."

The room falls silent again, the tension still lingering in the air. Our father lies between us, a silent witness to the rift that has grown over the years.

As our father drifts in and out of consciousness, his breathing shallow and labored, I stand, feeling the weight of the unresolved tension with Colton. It's clear that my presence is only adding to the strain.

"I should go," I say quietly, my eyes lingering on my father's frail form.

Colton doesn't look at me. His voice is cold, distant. "Maybe it's for the best. Don't bother coming back, Carter. It's clear where your priorities lie."

I want to argue, to defend myself, but the futility of it holds me back. "Colt, he's our father. Despite everything, I have a right to be here."

"Rights don't make you family, Carter. Presence does," Colton retorts, his eyes finally meeting mine, swirling with a mixture of anger and pain.

I exhale slowly, recognizing the truth in his words. "I'll keep in touch with the hospital," I say, offering a compromise, a way to stay informed without causing further discord.

Colton just nods, his gaze returning to our father. There's no goodbye, no acknowledgment as I turn and leave the room.

In the hallway, I pause, taking a moment to collect myself. The confrontation with Colton, the sight of my father so vulnerable, it's all too much. I lean against the wall, closing my eyes briefly.

After a moment, I find a nurse, seeking answers. "How bad is it?" I ask, my voice barely above a whisper.

She looks at me, her eyes kind yet somber. "It's serious. With his immune system compromised, it's about a fifty-fifty chance right now."

Her words hit me like a physical blow. Fifty-fifty. It's like flipping a coin on my father's life. A surge of emotions well up inside me—fear, regret, helplessness.

"Thank you," I manage to say, my throat tight.

As I walk away, her words echo in my mind. Fifty-fifty. The uncertainty of it all is overwhelming. I need to feel something definitive—fear, sorrow, hope—but instead, there's just a numbing confusion.

I step into the elevator, the doors closing with a soft ding. Alone in the descending box, the reality of my father's condition, my fractured relationship with Colton, and the unresolved tension with Megan swirl around me.

The elevator reaches the ground floor, and I step out into the bustling lobby, the noise and movement mirroring the whirlwind of thoughts going through my mind.

As I get in my car, I realize that I'm at a crossroads, not just in terms of my father's health, but in every aspect of my life. Everything feels precarious, barely balancing, like everything could come crashing down at any moment. I push all of my uncertainties aside and decide the time to take action is now.

Chapter Sixteen

Megan

At the Vivante Grand, the task of reorganizing the Barker-Davis wedding looms over me. I stand at the reception desk, speaking with Laura, who's being incredibly patient and helpful.

"I've managed to reorganize the caterer, thankfully," I explain, rifling through my notes. "But the cake... that's proving to be a nightmare after all the cancellations."

Laura nods sympathetically. "I'm sure you'll figure it out, Megan. You always do."

As I'm about to thank her, my gaze shifts to a familiar figure approaching. Tim. My heart skips a beat, and I instinctively turn away, hoping to avoid him. It's too late; he's already spotted me.

"Megan," he calls out, a casual smile on his face. "How's the wedding planning going? Your own wedding, I mean."

I stiffen, forcing a smile onto my face. "Oh, it's going... well. We're thinking of a small ceremony. Intimate, you know?"

He nods, his smile not quite reaching his eyes. "That sounds lovely. The venue—have you decided on that yet?"

I can feel Laura's curious gaze on us, and I scramble for a plausible answer. "We're still deciding, but we're thinking of having it here."

Tim's smile widens, but there's a sharpness to it that makes me uneasy. "Of course. Well, I'm sure it will be a beautiful event. Mr. Wright is a lucky man."

I thank him, my words feeling hollow. As I turn back to Laura, I can feel Tim's gaze on my back, and a shiver runs down my spine. His presence, his questions, they feel like a warning, a reminder that he's watching, waiting for his chance to interfere.

"Is everything okay, Megan?" Laura asks, her voice laced with concern.

I force a smile, nodding. "Yes, just a lot on my plate, but I'll manage."

"So, a small and intimate wedding, huh?" Tim says, leaning casually against the reception desk. Laura glares at him, but he continues. "Must be difficult to keep things low-key when you're engaged to someone like Carter Wright."

I feel a knot of tension forming in my stomach. "Well, we both value our privacy," I reply, trying to sound nonchalant.

Just then, Josh Warrington appears behind Tim, his presence like a dark cloud. Tim turns, greeting him with a nod. "Josh, perfect timing."

My heart sinks as I see them together. "Tim, why are you talking with a competitor?" I ask, unable to hide the suspicion in my voice.

Tim's expression shifts to one of smug satisfaction. "Oh, Josh and I have been having some interesting conversations lately. I'm considering a... change in my career path. Josh here has been very persuasive."

Josh Warrington steps forward, his eyes glinting with something akin to triumph. "Tim's been very helpful in providing insights into the Vivante Grand's operations. You know, insider information can be quite valuable."

Laura, sensing the growing tension, takes a step back, her eyes wide with concern. "I should get back to work," she murmurs, casting me a glance that clearly asks *are you okay?*

I nod, even as my gut twists into knots.

Tim leans in closer, his voice lowering. "See, Megan, together we've uncovered quite a bit of dirt on you and Carter. For one, that your engagement isn't real, and two, that this is all for money. Megan, what do you think your beloved clients would think about that information?

Josh cuts in, "We're reasonable men. We can be persuaded to keep this information to ourselves."

I feel a chill run down my spine. "What do you want, Tim?"

He smiles, a cold, calculating expression. "Compensation, of course. A little incentive to stay quiet."

Josh nods in agreement. "Think of it as... insurance."

This situation is quickly spiraling out of control, and I'm suddenly acutely aware of how dangerous this game has become. Tim and Josh joining forces could ruin not just the fake engagement but also our professional reputations.

"I need to talk to Carter about this," I say, trying to keep my voice steady.

Tim chuckles. "I'm sure you do, but don't take too long. We're not known for our patience."

As I walk away, my mind races with the implications of their threat. Carter needs to know about this immediately. This isn't just a petty rivalry or personal grudge anymore. It's a full-blown crisis, and we need to act fast before Tim and Josh make good on their threats.

I find a quiet corner in the hotel's lush garden, a space where I can message Carter without prying eyes. My fingers shake as I type, feeling the gravity of the situation.

Carter, we have a serious problem. Tim Donnelly and Josh Warrington are working together. Need to see you ASAP. I'm in the garden at the Grand.

His response is immediate. *On my way.*

True to his word, fifteen minutes later, Carter strides into the garden, his expression one of concern and urgency. He starts to demand answers, but I cut him off by closing the distance between us and pressing my lips to his. It's a spontaneous act, driven partly by the need to maintain our ruse and partly by my need for a momentary escape the stress.

The kiss is a mix of desperation and longing, our earlier encounter in the elevator still fresh in my mind. His lips are soft yet insistent against mine, and for a brief moment, all my worries fade into the background. The lingering desire from our previous embrace resurfaces, mingling with the anxiety of the present moment. It's a strange, intoxicating cocktail of emotions that leaves me feeling overwhelmed while yearning for more.

When we finally break apart, Carter looks at me, puzzled. "What was that for?" he asks, his voice husky.

"Why not?" I reply, trying to sound more confident than I feel.

He takes a deep breath, regaining his composure. "Where are Tim and Josh now?"

I shake my head, a sense of dread settling in my stomach. "I don't know. They left together, but they made their intentions clear. They're planning to use whatever they've found against us."

Carter's expression hardens. "I'll handle it."

I nod.

In the midst of the turmoil swirling around us, Carter shows a moment of tenderness that takes me by surprise. He reaches out, gently tucking a strand of hair behind my ear. His touch is soft, contrasting with the steely determination in his eyes.

His gaze holds mine, and I can see the worry there, the weight of our current situation. There's also determination, a quiet vow that he won't allow this situation to defeat us.

"Carter," I start, my voice wavering slightly.

He cuts me off with another kiss, this one initiated by him. It's a gentle, reassuring kiss, one that speaks more than words ever could. His lips move against mine with a tenderness that belies the strength of the emotions between us. The kiss deepens, and for a brief moment, all the complications fade away, leaving only the feeling of my heart fluttering in my chest.

As we pull apart, the question that's been burning in my mind almost slips out. What are we to each other? The words catch in my throat. Our situation is so complex, our relationship built on a foundation of pretense and necessity, yet colored with genuine feelings that neither of us seem fully ready to confront.

Carter looks at me, his expression softening. "We'll get through this, Megan," he says, his voice low and earnest. "I know it's a mess, but they won't win."

I nod, trying to find comfort in his words. "It's just... all of this," I gesture vaguely, encompassing everything from our fake engagement to the threats from Tim and Josh. "It's overwhelming."

He takes my hands in his, his hold firm. "I know, but I'm not going to let Tim or Josh, or anyone else, ruin what we've built. Not the business, not... not us."

I look up at him, touched by his protectiveness, by the sincerity in his eyes. It's the first time he's admitted that this is more than just our business arrangement.

"What is this between us, Carter?" The question slips out before I can stop it.

He hesitates, his gaze searching mine. There's a smile on his lips. Not quite a smirk, but something like it. "It's whatever we want it to be."

The honesty in his words brings a swell of relief within me. Our professional arrangement and personal emotions have intertwined, resulting in a bewildering yet honest bond.

"Well, that simplifies things, because I care about you far more than I probably should," I admit, feeling a mix of relief and apprehension at my own confession.

As I stand there, holding Carter's hands, the sunlight filtering through the leaves above us, I'm struck by his countenance. The natural light accentuates his features, casting a soft glow on his hair and warming his already tan skin.

The attraction and desire that have been simmering beneath the surface of our complicated relationship bubble up, impossible to ignore. I find myself drawn to him, not just by the gravity of our situation but by a genuine longing that I've been trying to suppress.

Acting on impulse, I reach up and gently tug at his collar, pulling him down to me. He doesn't resist and instead, wraps his arm around my waist, pulling me into him. Our lips meet in a kiss that's no longer about pretense or appearances, but about the raw desire warming between my thighs.

Carter kisses me back with an intensity that sends a thrill through me, his hand on my hip drawing me even closer. The world around us fades away, and for a moment, it's just the two of us, lost in each other.

Our moment of escape is abruptly interrupted when someone walks past us bringing with them the sudden realization that we're still in the middle of the hotel garden. The thought that anyone could be watching us sends a flush of embarrassment across my cheeks. I pull away, my heart still racing from the intensity of the kiss.

Carter looks equally flustered, a rare sight that makes him even more endearing. "We should probably be more careful," he says, his voice a little husky.

I nod, still trying to calm my racing heart. "Yeah, especially here."

There's a brief, awkward silence as we both try to regain our composure. It's clear that what's happening between us is no longer just a simple arrangement. The lines have been blurred, and now that we've admitted it, there's no going back.

Carter clears his throat, adjusting his collar. "I should get back to the office. We need to strategize about Tim and Josh."

"All right," I reply, sighing. "We can't let them get the upper hand."

As we walk back into the bustling hotel lobby, the reality of our situation settles back in. We have a crisis to manage, a threat to neutralize. Beneath it all, there's something else there now. Something I don't have a name for yet.

I steal a glance at Carter, his profile sharp against the sunlight. Whatever the future holds, it's clear that our relationship has evolved into something neither of us expected. As daunting as that might be, I can't deny the part of me that's excited to see where it leads.

We pass by the reception desk where Laura offers us a warm, knowing smile. Her gaze lingers on us for a moment, a silent acknowledgment of the bond she's just witnessed.

I pause, a thought crossing my mind. "Laura," I start, "if it came down to it, would you... would you be willing to help us as a witness? In case of legal action over this whole mess?"

Her smile is reassuring, unwavering. "Of course, Megan. You and Mr. Wright have always been good to us here."

Carter nods, a smile on his lips. "Thank you, Laura. I appreciate that."

As we move away from the desk, Carter muses aloud. "Maybe we should involve the police. It might be time to escalate this."

I feel a sudden surge of panic, my heart racing. "No, Carter, please," I say quickly, a little more forcefully than I intend. "No police, *please*."

"Why not?"

How can I tell him the truth? He knows about Brady, at least a little bit, but I don't know how to explain the fear of appearing in court, testifying against the very man that tormented me for weeks... Tim Donnelly reminds me too much of that time.

Instead of saying that, I murmur, "Just promise me. Please?"

Carter stops and looks at me, concern etched on his face. "All right, no police."

I nod, grateful for his understanding. "Thank you," I whisper, feeling a burden lift off my shoulders.

"We have a legal team looking into it," he adds. "We'll find another way to deal with Tim and Josh."

We continue walking in silence, each lost in our own thoughts. Our situation hangs heavily over us, casting an oppressive feeling in the air.

As we reach the doors, I glance back at Laura, still at her post. Her willingness to stand by us, to support us in whatever lies ahead, is a small beacon of hope in the midst of all the chaos.

Chapter Seventeen

Carter

For the rest of the day and well into the next, I'm distracted by the events at the Grand. The silence in my office is a stark contrast to the threatening chaos in my life. I find myself staring at my phone, contemplating whether to text Colton. But something holds me back. The tension between us, the unresolved issues, they all seem insurmountable.

My father's condition remains unchanged, without improvement. It leads me to question everything—the necessity of this charade with Megan, the whole façade we've built. It all seems so trivial in the grand scheme of things, especially if my father might not make it.

Lost in these thoughts, I barely notice the door opening until Megan appears in front of me holding a bag of sushi from a nearby restaurant.

"I thought we could have lunch together," she says, her voice soft, a welcome intrusion into my brooding thoughts.

"That sounds perfect," I reply, a small smile forming despite the turmoil inside me.

She sets the bag down on the table and starts unpacking the sushi. The simplicity of the act, her presence here, brings a sense of normalcy amidst the chaos of my life. It's a welcome reprieve.

As I watch her, the way she smiles, the way her eyes light up when she talks about small, everyday things, I realize she's become a significant part of my life.

We continue our meal, the sushi spread out between us. As we eat, I find myself wanting to understand Megan better, to bridge the gap that our arrangement has created.

"Megan," I start, my tone cautious, "about yesterday... When you asked me not to involve the police. I'm curious why."

She pauses, her chopsticks hovering over her plate. There's a hesitancy in her eyes, a vulnerability she doesn't often show. "It's... a long story," she begins, setting her chopsticks down.

She takes a deep breath. "You know about my ex. It turned ugly. He... he started stalking me."

The seriousness of her tone hits me, and I lean in, listening intently.

"He wouldn't leave me alone. Calls, messages, showing up at places... it got to a point where I had to take legal action. I had to go to court," she continues, her voice dropping to almost a whisper.

I reach over to her, covering her hand with mine. "That must have been tough."

She nods, a faraway look in her eyes. "Testifying against him was one of the hardest things I've ever done. Standing there, in front of everyone, having to relive every moment... "

"The worst part," she says, her voice tinged with bitterness, "he got away with just a restraining order. No real consequences. It felt like... like my ordeal meant nothing. That's why I didn't want the police involved. It's hard to trust a system that let you down."

I squeeze her hand gently, trying to offer comfort. "I'm sorry you had to go through that, Megan. We'll handle this thing our way then."

She offers me a small, grateful smile. "Thank you, Carter. That means a lot."

The intensity of Megan's experience, the rawness in her voice leaves me at a loss for words. I want to comfort her, to somehow ease the pain of her past, but I'm unsure how to do so. In the end, I default to what I know, what feels right in the moment—a kiss.

Leaning across the desk, I close the distance between us. The angle is awkward, our lips meeting in a clumsy yet earnest embrace. As our kiss deepens, the awkwardness fades away, replaced by a growing desire. The world outside this office, with all its complications and fears, recedes into the background.

As I pull away, Megan reaches out, her hand gently pulling me back. I smile, understanding her silent request. "Come here," I murmur, and she obliges, moving to sit on the edge of the desk in front of me.

I guide her legs to straddle me, bringing her closer, our bodies aligning in a more natural, intimate position. My hands slide up her skirt, grasping her thighs with a firmness that elicits a soft gasp from her. The sensation of her skin beneath my fingers sends a thrill through me, heightening the intensity of the moment.

Her reaction, the way she leans into my touch, encourages me. I tighten my grip slightly, enough to leave a mark, a physical reminder of *us*. Megan responds with a low sigh, her body pressing closer to mine.

The office, with its walls of books and framed awards, becomes our private escape. The kiss evolves from a simple gesture of comfort into something more passionate, more urgent. It's as if we're both trying to communicate what words cannot—our growing need for each other, the desire that has been steadily building between us.

Megan's hands find their way to my hair, tugging gently, her movements filled with a yearning that mirrors my own. The sound of our breathing, panting and breathless, fills the room.

Our embrace doesn't ease; instead, it intensifies. My hands, emboldened by her reactions, slide further up, exploring beneath her skirt. The feel of her skin under my fingertips is electric, sending a jolt of desire through me. She's soaked already, and I nudge her panties aside with my fingers.

Megan looks into my eyes, a playful yet sultry expression on her face. "Seems like you're getting quite comfortable with this arrangement," she teases, her breath warm against my lips.

I smirk, pressing closer to her. "I'm just adapting to the situation," I reply, my voice low.

Her response is to unbutton my pants, her movements deliberate yet teasing. She leans in to kiss me again, her lips moving against mine with a passion that matches my own growing fervor.

I find myself being rougher than usual, driven by a hot, heady desire as I slip inside of her. Megan responds in kind, meeting my intensity with her own, a low moan emanating from her full lips.

We fuck fast and hard, nothing but low gasps breaking the silence of the room. My hands grasp her thighs, squeezing with the rhythm of each thrust, Megan's arms tight around my waist.

Her hands roam freely, and I match her boldness, my own hands moving over her body with a possessiveness I hadn't allowed myself to express before. She feels beautiful beneath me, all silken skin that makes me pulse with excitement.

The intensity escalates, the air around us charged with unspoken promises. It's a release, a way to express the emotions that we've been holding back, not just today but over the weeks we've been together.

Megan comes a fraction before I do, clenching around me with a groan muffled as she presses her face into my neck. I gasp her name, hands tightening their grip as my orgasm shakes through me. I spill inside of her, hot and explosive, leaving us both breathless.

As we finally break apart, spent, there's a mutual understanding that what's happening between us is no longer just for show. It's real, and it's powerful.

We look at each other, our breaths mingling, the afterglow of our passion revealed in our flushed faces and bright eyes.

As I take a step back to admire Megan, righting my pants, I see her cheeks flushed a rosy hue and her hair tousled from our passionate embrace, and I feel a sense of awe. She's beautiful, her disarray only adding to her charm.

I reach out, attempting to tame her hair, but she laughs, swatting my hand away playfully. "Hey, I think you've done enough," she teases, her eyes sparkling with mischief.

"Just trying to help," I say with a chuckle, still breathless from our exertion.

"You have a funny way of helping," she retorts, her laughter light and infectious.

I can't remember the last time I felt this relaxed, this genuinely happy. For the first time in ages, my mind is calm, free from the worries that usually plague it.

I lean in and peck her nose, eliciting another laugh from her. She then comes to sit beside me, her presence a comforting warmth. We look at the remnants of our sushi lunch, now forgotten and pushed aside in the heat of the moment.

With an amused grin, Megan sweeps the remains into the trash. "Well, that was certainly one way to enjoy lunch," she comments.

"Definitely more enjoyable than eating," I reply, watching as she leans over the desk again, her fingers playfully tugging at my collar.

She looks up at me, a mischievous glint in her eyes. "You know, I could get used to lunches like this."

I laugh, a genuine, heartfelt sound. "This is the best lunch I've had in a long while."

Our eyes meet, and in them, I see not just desire, but a deepening connection, a shared understanding of the journey we've embarked on together. It's exhilarating and terrifying all at once.

Megan's hand finds mine, her fingers intertwining with mine in a gentle, comforting grip. "Whatever happens, I *really* hope we do this again," she says, her voice filled with conviction.

I squeeze her hand in response, grateful for her presence, for this unexpected turn our relationship has taken. "I think we should make it a regular occurrence."

In this quiet corner of the world, with Megan by my side, I feel a sense of peace and certainty I hadn't known I was missing. And as we prepare to face the challenges ahead, I know that with her, I'm ready for whatever comes our way.

Chapter Eighteen

Megan

Although I would willingly stay here forever, I know I can't. Glancing at Carter, I give my hair one last smooth over and peck him on the nose.

"You still look a mess," I tease him, straightening his collar with a flirtatious smile.

He grins back, a playful glint in his eyes. "I could say the same about you. It's a good look, though."

I laugh, feeling a warm glow at the easy banter between us. "I have to meet with Mr. Davis and Miss Barker now. I can't show up looking like I've just been... well, you know."

He steps closer, his voice dropping to a whisper. "Like you've been thoroughly wrecked by your fake fiancé?"

"Exactly that," I reply, my cheeks flushing with a mix of embarrassment and excitement.

Carter leans in and gives me a soft, lingering kiss at the door. "Good luck with your meeting," he says, his tone sincere but with an undercurrent of mischief.

"Thanks, I'll need it after this lunch break," I say, stepping into the elevator with a smile still on my lips.

The drive back to my office is uneventful, but my mind is far from calm. Memories of the passionate sex Carter and I shared in his office linger in my thoughts, making it hard to focus on my upcoming meeting.

When I arrive, Mr. Davis and Miss Barker are waiting for me outside my office. They both look eager and a little anxious, probably wondering about the status of their plans after the recent attempts to sabotage their wedding.

"Mr. Davis, Miss Barker, please come in," I greet them, ushering them into my office with a professional smile.

As I lead them inside, I feel a sense of satisfaction. Despite the chaos in my personal life, I'm still managing to keep my professional world running smoothly. Beneath that professional exterior, a part of me is still back in Carter's office, with his hands all over me and cock deep inside me...

As we sit down to discuss their wedding arrangements, I force myself to keep focused on the conversation at hand. The contrast between my professional and personal life has never been so profound, and yet I find myself relishing the complexity of it all.

I happily share the progress I've made with my clients, "I've managed to rebook the catering with the same company, and I'm currently working on the cake and a few other details. I'm confident everything will be ready in time for your original date," I explain, trying to instill a sense of confidence and control.

Miss Barker's face brightens with relief. "That's wonderful news, Miss Medina. We really appreciate all your hard work."

However, Mr. Davis's expression is far from pleased. "What about finding out who did this?" he asks sharply. "Rebooking is fine, but it doesn't solve the root of the problem."

I'm taken aback by his intensity. "Well, we are looking into that," I start, but he cuts me off.

"This is completely unprofessional. Fixing the problem isn't enough. We need to know who's responsible and ensure they're punished. How can we feel confident in the success of our wedding if we don't know who's trying to sabotage it?"

Miss Barker places a hand on his arm, trying to calm him. "Darling, let's focus on the positives. Miss Medina is doing her best."

Mr. Davis is undeterred, his frustration evident. "No, this is important. We can't just brush it under the rug."

I realize I need to de-escalate the situation quickly. "Mr. Davis, I completely understand your concerns, and I assure you, we are taking this very seriously," I say with a calming tone. "My team and I are doing everything we can to investigate the matter. Our goal is not only to ensure your wedding goes smoothly but also to maintain the integrity and security of the entire process."

He seems slightly mollified by my reassurance but remains tense. "I just want to make sure this doesn't happen again," he says, his voice softer now.

"Absolutely," I reply, nodding. "I promise to keep you both updated on any developments. Our priority is your peace of mind and the success of your wedding."

The rest of the meeting proceeds smoothly with me outlining the revised plans and timelines. Despite the earlier tension, I manage to bring the focus back to the upcoming celebration, reassuring them of my commitment to making their day as special as they envision.

After they leave, I'm exhausted. Balancing the demands of my clients with the ongoing issues with Tim and Josh is proving to be more challenging than I anticipated. Despite the hurdles, I'm determined to stay on top of things. My reputation and the happiness of my clients depend on it.

I take a moment to gather my thoughts. The Barker-Davis wedding is back on track, which is a relief, but there's still so much to handle. My own supposed wedding, the looming threats from Tim and Josh—it feels like I'm juggling too many balls, and I can't afford to let any of them drop.

Tim and Josh's silence is particularly unnerving. Their absence of communication only heightens my anxiety. What are they planning? When will they make their next move, and what will it be?

Lost in these thoughts, my phone buzzes with a message from Carter. I open it, hoping for some word on our current predicament, but instead, I find something entirely different.

We should set a date for our wedding. How about in three weeks? The eighteenth.

I stare at the message, perplexed. Three weeks? That's incredibly soon. Why the rush? Is it related to his father's health, or is there another reason he's not mentioning? I quickly type a response.

Why so soon? Is everything okay?

There's no immediate reply. The message hangs there, unanswered, adding another layer of uncertainty to the already complex situation.

I lean back in my chair, my mind racing. A fake wedding in three weeks—it's not just the logistics that worry me, but the implications. What does this accelerated timeline mean for our arrangement? For the threats from Tim and Josh?... For the real feelings developing between Carter and me?

The more I think about it, the more it feels like we're hurtling toward something unavoidable, something that could either solidify our strange relationship or blow it into pieces. The line between our professional arrangement and the personal feelings has been growing fuzzier by the day.

I look around my office, at the wedding plans and notes scattered across my desk, a physical manifestation of the chaos in my life. The juxtaposition of planning someone else's happily ever after while my own personal and professional life teeters on the brink isn't lost on me.

With no reply from Carter, I decide to focus on what I can control. There's still plenty of work to be done for the Barker-Davis wedding and immersing myself in those details might be the distraction I need. But even as I dive into my work, part of my mind remains fixated on Carter's message and the myriad of questions it raises.

The buzz of my phone with a new message momentarily pulls me from my swirling thoughts. It's from Melissa, asking if I'm free to go out for drinks. I pause, reflecting on how distant I've been lately. Between the chaotic wedding planning and my arrangement with Carter, I've hardly had time for anything else, let alone spending time with my family.

I glance at my calendar, cluttered with appointments and reminders, then back at Melissa's message. Guilt washes over me. Melissa has always been there for me, and I've been neglecting our relationship amidst the tumult of my professional and personal life.

I quickly type a response, accepting her invitation. Maybe a night out with Melissa is exactly what I need—a chance to unwind, to get away from the stress and complications that have been dominating my life. Family time might offer the respite I desperately need.

As I send the message, however, my mind drifts back to the looming threat of Josh and Tim. Their silence is unsettling, like the calm before a storm. I can't shake the feeling that they're planning something, biding their time before they strike.

A realization hits me—I can't just sit back and wait for them to make their move. I need to confront this head-on, on my own terms. Maybe it's time I approach Tim and Josh myself, find out exactly what they want and how to stop them.

With this new resolve, I start to strategize. I'll need to be careful, ensure I don't put Carter or myself in a more precarious situation. The thought of taking control, of not being at the mercy of their games is empowering.

The rest of the day is spent in a blur of work and planning. I finalize details for the Barker-Davis wedding while also contemplating how to handle the confrontation with Tim and Josh. It's a delicate balance, but I'm determined to manage it.

As evening approaches, I prepare to meet Melissa. Our night out is a much-needed break, a chance to reconnect with my sister and momentarily escape the chaos. In the back of my mind, the plan to face Tim and Josh lingers, a constant reminder that this brief respite is just that—brief.

I leave the office with mixed feelings—the excitement of seeing Melissa and the apprehension of the confrontation that awaits me. One thing is clear: I'm not going to let Tim and Josh control the narrative anymore. It's time to take the reins and deal with this, once and for all.

Arriving at Melissa's place, I'm greeted with a warm smile and a comforting hug. It's a welcome change from the tension and uncertainty that have been clouding my days. Melissa's home is cozy and inviting.

As we settle in, Melissa casually asks, "So, how's the wedding planning going?"

Instinctively, I start to talk about the Barker-Davis wedding, detailing the recent hiccups and how I've managed to keep things on track. It's only when Melissa interrupts me with a gentle laugh that I realize my mistake.

"No, I meant your wedding, Megan. You and Carter Wright," she clarifies, a hint of surprise in her voice.

"Oh, right. That," I say.

"I have to admit, I was surprised when I heard about it. You and Carter Wright... It's all so fast. Carter, of all people, considering he and I used to be a thing."

I smile awkwardly, trying to ignore the guilt settling in my gut. "Yeah, I know you two dated in college. I was always too studious back then to bother with dating."

"Mmm," Melissa hums as she leads me into the living room. "The two of us were so in love, I thought for sure I'd be the one marrying him. Funny, how things turn out. He ended us. I went on to grad school."

The revelation hits me like a physical blow. I knew Melissa and Carter had a brief history together, but I never knew the depth of their relationship. In love? The word echoes in my mind, a painful reminder of how little I actually know about Carter's past.

"Wait... You were in love with him?" I ask, my voice barely above a whisper, feeling a sense of betrayal washing over me.

Melissa nods, a distant look in her eyes. "Yes, but it was a long time ago. We were young, and it was intense. Too bad Carter was too ambitious, he didn't want to rebel against his father's priorities and broke us off."

I stand there, stunned, trying to process this new information. All this time, I've been growing closer to Carter, believing in what we've been building, yet I was oblivious to this significant part of his past. The fact that he never mentioned it, never shared this piece of himself with me, stings.

"Why didn't you tell me?" I ask, feeling a mix of hurt and confusion.

Melissa sighs. "I thought you knew, Megan. It was years ago, and I'm over it now. I'm happy for you, honestly, I just want you to be careful."

"Well, I didn't know."

Melissa sighed. "Evidently."

There's more I want to say, and without thinking I blurt, "For someone in love, you didn't act like it."

"Sometimes love isn't enough. I needed him more than he needed me, and he ended things. It was better that we went no-contact."

I believe her. It hurts, but I do. "Still," I say, "I never realized how deep your feelings went for him."

She takes a deep breath before responding, "Well, I never told you. I never even told *him*."

It shouldn't matter, and yet I can't shake the discomfort of betrayal.

Chapter Nineteen

Carter

At home, I'm lost in thought, contemplating the situation with Megan, Tim, and Josh, when the intercom buzzes. It's Megan, her voice tinged with an emotion I can't quite place. She sounds upset, urgent. Without hesitation, I buzz her in.

Moments later, she storms into my apartment, her eyes ablaze with a mix of anger and hurt. "Were you in love with Melissa when you were younger?" she demands, cutting straight to the heart of the matter.

Her question catches me off guard. Yes, there was a time when I loved Melissa, but it was a different kind of love, born of youth and naiveté. I was a different person back then, more self-centered, more concerned with my own ambitions.

"Megan, I—" I start, faltering, trying to find the right words.

"Why didn't you tell me?" she interrupts, her voice rising. "I always thought it was just a fling, but she said you were in love."

Megan's question hangs heavily in the air, charged with emotion. Her revelation about Melissa catches me off guard, creating a tension that quickly escalates.

"Was it always fake to you, Carter?" Megan's voice is sharp, cutting through the silence of my apartment.

I feel a surge of frustration, folding my arms across my chest. "Melissa and I were complicated," I retort, my voice rising despite my attempts to keep calm. "Why does it matter if I was in love with Melissa? That was a long time ago."

"Because she's my sister, Carter! Don't you think I have a right to know these things?"

"That's not fair, Megan. You know this started as a pretense. We never agreed to bring personal histories into it."

"It's different now, isn't it? Or was I just imagining that there was more between us?" Her voice breaks slightly, revealing a vulnerability beneath her anger.

"Yes, things have changed, but that doesn't change why we went into this in the first place."

"So, that's it, then? We just ignore whatever is happening between us because it wasn't part of the original deal?" she challenges, her eyes searching mine for something, some sign of my true feelings.

"What do you want me to say? I didn't bring it up because I didn't think it mattered."

Her expression hardens. "Maybe it's time for you to figure it out, Carter, because I'm not going to be part of some game where I'm the last to know the rules. It's not just about you having a history with Melissa. It's that you kept it from me, that you never thought it was important to tell me."

I stand my ground, though I can feel the tension building inside me. "Megan, it was forever ago. Why does it matter who I was involved with before this?"

"It matters to me!" she exclaims, her frustration palpable. "I thought... I thought we were building something here, beyond the arrangement. Clearly, I was mistaken."

"We can't just change the rules midway. I never promised this would be anything more," I say, my frustration building.

Megan shakes her head, her expression a mix of anger and disbelief. "The rules *changed* the first time this started feeling like something genuine."

Frustrated and hurt, Megan turns and storms out of my apartment. I follow her into the hall, my own emotions a tangled mess. "Megan, wait," I call out, but she stops and turns, her expression one of finality.

"No, Carter. Just... leave it. I need some space right now."

She walks away, leaving me standing in the hallway, watching her go. A creeping sense of guilt washes over me. She's right—it was all supposed to be fake, a mere charade. So why do I feel this pang of guilt, this sense of loss as she walks away?

I stand there for a moment longer, trying to make sense of my feelings. The realization that what I feel for Megan might be more than just the convenience of our arrangement is unsettling. It challenges everything I thought this was going to be, everything I thought I wanted.

Slowly making my way back into my penthouse, I sit down, thinking hard. I was so certain that I could keep this professional, keep it within the boundaries we had set. Now, I'm not sure we will even be able to see it through to the end. That uncertainty is more frightening than I care to admit.

Chapter Twenty

Megan

I'm standing outside Melissa's door, apprehensive but ready. After the heated exchange with Carter, my thoughts keep circling back to Melissa and our conversation about him. I need to set things right with her, to clear the air.

Taking a deep breath, I knock on the door. Melissa answers, her expression softening when she sees me. "Megan," she says, stepping aside to let me in. "I wasn't expecting you."

"I need to talk," I say, stepping into the familiar warmth of her home.

We sit down in her living room, the comfortable space a stark contrast to the tension I feel. "Melissa, I'm sorry about earlier. I shouldn't have reacted the way I did about Carter," my voice tinged with regret.

Melissa waves a hand dismissively. "Megan, it's okay. I understand it must have been a shock. Carter and I, that was a lifetime ago. It has no bearing on now."

"But it does," I insist, looking down at my hands. "I... I shouldn't have been such a bitch."

Melissa reaches out, her hand covering mine. "Megan, people change, they move on. Honestly, I think your reaction was pretty normal."

I look up at her, her words offering a perspective I hadn't considered. "I just feel like I'm falling into something I can't control. Falling for him."

"Falling for him, as in...?"

I nod, the words spilling out. "I think I might be falling in love with Carter. This was all supposed to be a simple arrangement, but now... "

Melissa's brows furrow. "Arrangement?"

Oh. I've said too much but now... but what's the point in lying anymore? It's time to come clean.

"Please, don't be angry... Carter needed to marry someone to earn his father's inheritance, and I thought it would look good for my clients if I was engaged to someone like Carter. Maybe it was a chance to be with someone that would typically never be seen with me."

I expect anger. An outburst. Except, Melissa only sighs and takes my hand, her expression understanding. "You did a stupid thing, Megan, but I think you've suffered enough for it."

"You're not..."

"No, I'm not."

Relief floods through me so strongly that for a moment, I forget how to breathe. When I finally do manage to speak, my voice is halting. "Thank you."

"So, you're really in love with him?"

"I... yes, I am."

Melissa squeezes my hand. "Love has a way of sneaking up on us, especially when we least expect it. That's not a bad thing. It's what makes life so unpredictable and beautiful."

"What if he doesn't feel the same way? What if this all blows up in my face?" The fear in my voice is obvious.

"You won't know unless you open up to him, Megan. You both need to be honest with each other, about how you feel, about what you want from this," Melissa advises, her voice full of empathy. "Whatever happens, I know you're strong enough to get through it."

I nod, feeling a surge of gratitude. "It's just all been so overwhelming. I really appreciate your support and understanding."

Just then, my phone buzzes with a message from Carter, breaking the moment. I open the text, my heart sinking as I read the words.

My father's taken a turn for the worse. I'm heading to the hospital now. This whole arrangement won't matter anymore if he doesn't make it.

The message is grim, almost harsh, and it leaves me feeling cold. Carter's pain is evident, but so is the brutal reality of our situation.

Melissa notices the change in my expression. "What is it, is everything okay?"

I hand her the phone, letting her read the message. She hands it back with a sympathetic look. "It sounds like he's hurting."

I sigh, feeling a mix of concern and confusion. "It sounds like he's only worried about his inheritance."

Melissa leans in, her voice gentle. "Maybe that's his way of coping, Megan. People sometimes retreat into what they know best when they're hurting."

I consider her words, knowing there's truth in them. Carter has always been business-focused, and it makes sense that he'd revert to that mindset in times of stress.

"What does that mean for us though?" I ask, more to myself than to Melissa. "If his father... if he doesn't make it, do we just... go back to being strangers?"

Melissa takes my hand again. "You'll cross that bridge when you come to it. For now, just be there for him. He's going through a lot."

I nod, knowing she's right. Despite the uncertainty and the harshness of his message, Carter is facing the potential loss of his father. He needs support, not conflict.

"I should probably go to him," I say, standing up. "He shouldn't be alone at a time like this."

Melissa stands as well, giving me a supportive hug. "Go. Be with him. Whatever happens, you'll figure it out."

Leaving Melissa's place, I am filled with a renewed purpose. My relationship with Carter might be complicated, but right now, he needs someone, and I can be that person. As I head to the hospital, I'm determined to stand by Carter, to face whatever comes our way, together.

When I arrive at the hospital, the sterile environment feels cold and unwelcoming. After asking for directions, I make my way to the ward where Carter's father is being treated. The hospital's quiet corridors echo with the low hum of medical equipment and hushed conversations, adding to the gravity of the situation.

I find Carter outside a private hospital room, his back to the wall, lost in thought. The room, no doubt, costs a considerable sum, indicative of his father's status and Carter's ability to provide the best care.

Seeing him there, a mix of emotions courses through me—concern, apprehension, and a deep urge to comfort him. "Carter," I say softly as I approach.

He looks up, surprise and irritation flicker across his face. "Megan? What are you doing here?"

"I was worried," I reply, taking a cautious step closer. "How's your father?"

He looks away, his jaw clenched. "Not doing well," he snaps, his voice betraying his hurt.

I pause, unsure of how to proceed. It's clear that Carter is having a tough time, burdened by his father's condition. Yet, he's putting up walls, unwilling to show just how affected he is.

"Listen, we need to speed up our arrangement," he says abruptly, changing the subject. "We can't wait any longer."

His sudden shift back to our arrangement catches me off guard. "Carter, is this really the time to talk about that?"

He looks back at me, his expression hard. "It's exactly the time. We need to move forward with this, now more than ever."

I search his face, trying to understand his urgency. "You should be focusing on him, not that."

For a moment, he's silent, then he lets out a heavy sigh, his resolve crumbling ever so slightly. "And if he dies before I can complete my side of the deal?"

"There's more to life than *money*, Carter!"

I see frustration bubbling under the surface. "That was the whole point of all of this. If—if it all fails now, what was the point of any of it?"

"Are you seriously thinking about your inheritance right now?"

Carter scowls, but then his face softens. "I don't even know if I care about that anymore," he admits quietly, almost to himself. "It's not really about the inheritance. I don't need it. It's about Dad's approval. I've always tried to live up to his terms, even though I fought him on all of them."

I can see the shift as he begins to surrender to his true emotions. I step closer, my heart aching for him. "Carter, talk to me. What's really going on?"

He shakes his head, looking back at the closed door of his father's room. "I just... I need something to focus on, something to keep me going. This arrangement... it's something I can control."

I understand then—him clinging to our arrangement is a lifeline amid the chaos, a semblance of control in an uncontrollable situation.

Reaching out, I gently place a hand on his arm. "I'm here, Carter. Whatever you need."

He doesn't respond, but he doesn't pull away either. We stand there in silence, the seriousness of his father's condition looming over us.

In the somber quiet of the hospital corridor, I act on impulse, stepping closer to Carter. I can see the turmoil in his eyes, the battle between maintaining control and letting go. Without a word, I lean in and kiss him.

The kiss is different from any we've shared before. It's not fueled by passion or desire but by a deep, aching need for understanding. My lips press against his softly, tentatively at first, but then with more urgency, attempting to convey all the emotions swirling inside me. His response is hesitant, but then he yields, the desperation in his kiss matching mine.

As we pull away, our breaths mingling, I look into his eyes, searching for some sign of what he's thinking, feeling. "Carter," I begin, my voice barely above a whisper. "Maybe we should put our arrangement on hold for now. Focus on your father."

He looks at me, a mixture of relief and something else—perhaps disappointment—flickering in his eyes. "You might be right," he says, his voice hoarse. "It's just... everything's so uncertain right now."

I nod, understanding. "We can figure all of that out later, once things have settled."

There's a pause, a moment of shared silence, before he speaks again. "I've never really gotten along with my father," he admits, his voice laden with sadness and a longing I hadn't heard before. "Now, the thought of him dying... it's making me realize how much I've lost, how much I never had."

The vulnerability in his admission tugs at my heart. I reach out, taking his hand in mine. "It's never easy, facing the mortality of a parent, especially when you have a complicated relationship."

He squeezes my hand, a small gesture of gratitude. "I don't think the reality of the situation has settled in yet."

I squeeze his hand back, offering what comfort I can. "You're not alone, Carter. I'm here."

In the quiet of the hospital corridor, a look of hesitancy crosses Carter's face, as if he's wrestling with something he wants to say. I notice the subtle shift in his expression, the way his eyes linger on mine, filled with an unspoken message.

"Carter, if there's something you want to say, you can tell me," I encourage gently, sensing the gravity of whatever is on his mind.

He looks around the corridor, the clinical setting seemingly stifling whatever he's trying to express. "Not here," he says, a hint of urgency in his voice. "Let's go outside."

We make our way to the hospital garden, a serene space with neatly manicured lawns and a scattering of benches beneath sprawling trees. It's a stark contrast to the sterile environment of the hospital, offering a semblance of peace and normalcy.

We find a secluded spot under a large tree, its branches providing a canopy of leaves that rustle softly in the breeze. The outdoor setting seems to ease some of the tension between us, the open air a welcome respite from the confining walls of the hospital.

Carter takes a deep breath, steeling himself. I watch him, my heart pounding in anticipation. The look on his face, the seriousness in his eyes, it all points to something significant, something potentially life-altering.

As he turns to face me, I brace myself, questions racing through my mind. Is he going to reject me? To say that our arrangement is still purely business, void of any real emotions? The fear of what he might say is almost paralyzing.

I need to know. Whatever he has to say, I'm ready to face it, even if it's not what I hope to hear. The uncertainty, the not knowing—it's been a shadow hanging over us, and it's time to bring it into the light.

Chapter Twenty-One

Carter

Sitting there beneath the tree, with Megan looking at me in a mix of anticipation and fear, I realize that this is the moment of truth. This is where I lay everything on the line, where I confess what I've been trying to deny even to myself.

"Megan," I start, my voice barely above a whisper, "I have a confession to make." I pause, gathering my thoughts, struggling to maintain my composure. "I'm in love with you."

The words hang in the air between us, a confession that's both terrifying and liberating. I look into her eyes, trying to gauge her reaction, while a part of me braces for rejection.

"This might have started as something fake, a simple arrangement," I continue, my voice growing stronger with each word. "It's not anymore. Not to me."

I can feel my guise slipping, the walls I've built around my emotions crumbling. "I don't care about the consequences anymore—the inheritance, my family's disapproval. None of that matters. All that matters is that I love you, Megan. Being with you... it's made me see things differently. You've made me see things differently."

I reach out, taking her hands in mine, needing the physical connection to affirm my confession. "I know this is a lot to take in, and I don't expect you to say anything right away. I just needed you to know, to understand how I feel."

Megan looks at me, a multitude of emotions flickering across her face as she processes my confession. For a moment she's silent, my heart races, bracing for her response, fearing the worst.

Finally, she speaks, her voice soft yet full of emotion mirroring my own. "Carter, I... I love you too."

Her words are like a balm to my anxious heart. "You do?" I ask in disbelief.

"Yes, I do," she affirms, her eyes shining with sincerity. "I've been trying to deny it, to keep it all professional and under control. Every moment with you, every laugh, every argument, it's made me realize how much you mean to me."

I can feel a smile spreading across my face, a sense of relief and happiness washing over me. "I wasn't sure."

She squeezes my hands, her grip reassuring. "Carter, you've brought something into my life that I didn't even know was missing. I want to be with you, for real, not just as part of some arrangement."

I lean in, capturing her lips in a kiss that's filled with a new intensity, a celebration of our mutual confession. The kiss is deep, passionate, it sends a thrill through me as I pull her against me.

As we pull away, Megan is smiling, her face radiant with joy. "So, what does this mean for us?" she asks, a playful note in her voice.

I take a deep breath, feeling a sense of purpose and direction I hadn't felt before. "It means I want our relationship to be real, if you'll have me. Not just a pretense for the sake of my father's will, but something genuine, something based on how we truly feel about each other."

Her smile widens, and she nods. "Of course, I'll have you, Carter. I want this, us, to be real more than anything."

We sit there under the tree, the world around us fading into the background. It's just the two of us, united in our newfound love and commitment to each other. The challenges we face haven't disappeared—my father's health, the threats from Tim and Josh—but they now seem surmountable, manageable even, with Megan by my side.

I wrap an arm around Megan's shoulder, drawing her closer. She leans into me, her presence a comforting warmth against the evening chill. A couple walking past glances at us curiously, but I barely notice.

I break the comfortable silence. "I want to tell my father about us, about everything."

Megan looks at me, uncertainty in her eyes. "Are you sure? Now, with everything that's happening?"

I nod. "It's something I want to do. I don't want to pretend. He needs to know the truth, about the will, about us."

She reaches up, her hand gently caressing my cheek. "If that's what you want to do, then I support you."

I feel a surge of gratitude for her understanding and encouragement. "Thank you, Megan. There's something else—we need to take care of Josh and Tim. We can't let them continue to hold these threats over us."

She nods in agreement, her expression determined. "You're right. We'll handle them together."

With a newfound sense of purpose, we stand up and make our way back to the hospital room. As we walk, I feel a mixture of nerves and determination. I've never been truly honest with my father, always maintaining the facade of a dutiful son. Now, with Megan by my side, I feel ready to face him, to speak truthfully.

We reach my father's room, and I take a deep breath before opening the door. Inside, the soft beeping of the medical equipment is a steady background noise. My father looks frail, a stark contrast to the strong, imposing figure he once was.

"Dad," I begin, my voice steady. "I want you to meet someone. This is Megan."

Megan steps forward, offering a warm, albeit tentative, smile. My father's eyes flicker with a mixture of curiosity and surprise.

"I brought her here to tell you something important," I continue, taking Megan's hand in mine. "At first, our relationship was just a part of an arrangement, to fulfill the conditions of your will. Things have changed." I pull her against my side, and she glances up at me with a smile of encouragement.

In the stillness of the hospital room, my father looks at Megan and me, his expression hard to read. There's a long, heavy silence before he finally speaks, his voice weak but laced with disappointment.

"Carter, I never thought you'd be the type to fake a relationship for money or my approval," he says, the words heavy with judgment.

Megan steps forward, her voice firm yet respectful. "Mr. Wright, with all due respect, what started as an arrangement has turned into something genuine. Carter isn't doing this for your money or your approval. He's doing it because he cares about me, and I care about him."

My father's eyes shift to Megan, then back to me. "Is this true, Carter? Are you really with her because you want to be, not because of my conditions?"

I nod, feeling a surge of resolve. "Yes, Dad. It's true. What Megan and I have... it's real. I'm with her because she makes me happy, something I haven't felt in a long time."

162

There's a moment of silence as my father processes what I've said. Then, his voice tinged with bitterness, he speaks again. "So, my approval, my legacy, it means nothing to you?"

I take a deep breath, feeling Megan's supportive presence beside me. "Dad, I've spent my whole life trying to earn your approval, to live up to your expectations. I've realized that I need to live for myself, for my own happiness. I hope you get better, but I'm done trying to be someone I'm not, just to please you."

The room is filled with a tense silence following my words. My father looks away, a pained expression crossing his features. It's clear that my words have hit a nerve, but I know it's a necessary confrontation, a step toward my own independence and happiness.

Megan gently squeezes my hand, her silent support speaking volumes. We stand together, a united front in the face of my father's disapproval.

After a few moments, my father speaks again, his voice softer, almost resigned. "I see. Perhaps I've been wrong about a few things. About you, Carter."

His admission is not a full acceptance, but it's a start, an acknowledgment of the changes in me. As we leave the room, I feel a weight lifted off my shoulders. The future is still uncertain, and my father's health remains a concern, but for the first time, I feel free from the burden of his expectations.

Megan and I walk down the hospital corridor, hand in hand, stepping into a future that we'll shape on our own terms, together.

Megan turns to me, her eyes reflecting a mix of emotions—relief, affection, and a hint of bold determination. Without a word, she reaches up and pulls me into a kiss.

Her lips meet mine with a passion that takes my breath away. The kiss is eager, intense, a culmination of the emotions and confessions we've just shared. I match her intensity, wrapping my arms around her, drawing her closer. The world around us fades into a blur as we lose ourselves in the kiss, in the connection that we've solidified.

Our kiss deepens, fueled by the release of pent-up emotions and the realization of our mutual feelings. There's an urgency to our movements, a desperate need to express everything we've been holding back.

As the intensity grows, Megan suddenly pulls away, a flush of embarrassment coloring her cheeks. "I'm sorry," she stammers, "I just got carried away. We're in a public space."

I can't help but smile, touched by her spontaneity and the depth of her feelings. "Don't apologize," I say softly. "It was perfect."

There's a sparkle in her eyes, a mixture of happiness and a hint of mischief. "Well, we certainly made a statement," she says with a light laugh.

I pull her into a gentle embrace, feeling a sense of contentment and hope. "Thank you, Megan, for being here with me, for supporting me through this. It means more than you know."

She hugs me back, her head resting against my chest. "Of course Carter, we're in this together."

We stand there for a moment, savoring the comfort of each other's presence. Then, hand in hand, we walk out of the hospital, stepping into the cool evening air. The challenges that lie ahead seem less daunting together.

As we walk to the car, I feel a sense of lightness, a freedom from the constraints that have held me back. With Megan by my side, I'm ready to face whatever comes our way. Our relationship may have started as a pretense, but now it's something real, something profound.

The drive back is quiet, but it's a comfortable silence, filled with an unspoken understanding and our shared anticipation for the future. As I glance at Megan, her profile illuminated by the streetlights passing by, I realize how lucky I am to have her in my life.

Chapter Twenty-Two

Megan

Standing outside the meeting room at the Vivante Grand two days later, I'm both nervous and determined. Inside, Tim and Josh are probably plotting their next move, and I'm about to confront them. It's daunting, but it's something I need to do.

As I'm rehearsing what to say in my head, Melissa arrives, her presence immediately comforting. Successfully managing dozens of research teams in her lab means she's a deft manager of people, and of reading them. She's here to act as a mediator and, if things go south, a witness. "Ready for this?" she asks, her voice steady.

I nod, trying to muster confidence. "As ready as I'll ever be. Thanks for being here, Melissa. It means a lot."

She smiles reassuringly. "You're not alone in this, Megan. We'll handle them together."

We exchange a few more words, Melissa offering support and advice, helping to steady my fraying nerves. As we're talking, Carter appears. The moment he sees Melissa and I together, there's a brief flash of uncertainty in his expression.

"Carter," I greet him, trying to ease the tension. "You're right on time. Did you see my text about Melissa joining us?"

He nods, and casts Melissa and I a half-smile. "Melissa, are you sure you want to get involved in this?"

Melissa steps forward, offering a polite smile. "It's good to see you, Carter. I'm here to support Megan, as an observer, mediator only if necessary. Don't worry. Megan's got this."

Carter nods, the moment of awkwardness passing as he turns his attention back to me. "Are you ready for this?"

Taking a deep breath, I feel a renewed sense of purpose. "Yes. Let's do this."

Together, the three of us stand outside the meeting room. I take a moment to collect my thoughts before opening the door. Inside, Tim and Josh are seated at the table, looking surprised to see not only me but Melissa as well.

"Good morning, gentlemen," I start, my voice stronger than I feel. "We need to talk about the recent issues regarding my client's wedding arrangements and your involvement in them."

Tim raises an eyebrow, a smirk forming on his lips. "Megan, you brought a little entourage, I see."

Josh looks less amused, his expression one of cautious interest. "What exactly are you accusing us of, Megan?"

I step forward, Melissa and Carter flanking me. "It's not an accusation, it's a fact. We know you've been trying to sabotage my business, amongst other things."

"I have no idea what you're talking about, Megan," Josh says with a dismissive wave of his hand. "And even if you did have some kind of proof to this accusation, I'm wealthy enough to handle any civil court case. So, go on, get to your point."

I hold my ground, bolstered by the support of Melissa and Carter at my sides. "This isn't about taking you to civil court, Josh," I reply firmly. "We have witnesses to your interference—the Vivante's receptionist, and my clients, Mr.

Davis and Miss Barker. If you both don't back off, this won't just be a civil matter. We're prepared to make it a criminal one."

Josh's expression hardens, but he maintains his denial. "This is all hearsay and conjecture. You have no proof."

I can feel the tension in the room rising, but I refuse to back down. "Tim, you have a distinctive voice and you do not sound like Landon Davis. Suppliers you canceled have identified your voice. We have enough to make a case, Josh. We know you have it out for Carter and me. With the resources at Carter's disposal, do you really want to take that risk?"

Josh scowls. "You think I can't pay the courts off? You'd be amazed at what a little money can do."

"You say that," Carter states, "I'm sure you've done it before, even; but when it comes to money and power, Josh, I outnumber you on both accounts."

Josh wilts slightly but doesn't back down. "If you take this to court, I'll ruin you. Take you for everything you're worth and more. Vivante hotels will be *mine*."

"Will they, now?"

"Yes, and I'll ruin your little fiancée's career as well. All my friend Tim here wanted was a chance to be with Megan. But me... I'm after so much more."

Melissa and Carter both offer me a look of support. Carter can barely contain his smirk, and Melissa's poker face isn't much better.

"This whole time, you've wanted to tear down the Vivante empire," I say, "I think that sounds like a threat."

"You're damn right it is."

And that's all that any of us needs to hear. With a flourish, I pull my cell phone out of my pocket and click *end recording*.

As I do, Josh's face pales. "You can't do that!"

Tim glances nervously at Josh, then back at me. It's clear he's less confident in their position than Josh is. "What do you want, Megan?" he asks, his voice barely above a whisper.

"It's simple," I say, locking eyes with Josh. "Stop your attempts to sabotage my business and my clients. It's obvious this has turned into some petty revenge plot, Tim, and I'm not interested in you at all. While we're at it, leave Carter and his business alone. If I even get a hint of you interfering again, we'll take everything we have to the authorities."

I see the surprise in Carter's face, echoed in the thud of my own pulse. After I asked Carter not to involve the police, he knows this is a big threat.

Josh leans back in his chair, assessing the situation. "We still have dirt on you, Megan. We know your engagement is fake, I can still tell everyone... "

"Sure," I blurt out, "go ahead."

I could explain why I don't care. Tell them that Carter and I are together for real now. Except, they don't deserve the time or effort it would take to explain; all they need to know is that Carter and I aren't hiding anymore.

To prove my point, I take Carter's hand and offer a gentle squeeze.

Josh stiffens in his seat. After a long moment, he sighs, his expression unreadable. "Alright, Megan. You've made your point. We'll back off."

I don't fully trust his acquiescence, but it's a start. "Good. I'll hold you to that."

"Tim," I say, holding his gaze, "I'm aware of your... obsession with me and it ends now. Any more inappropriate behavior, and not only will you face legal repercussions, but I'll also ensure you're reported to the appropriate authorities in the hospitality industry."

Carter steps forward, his tone firm. "I should have had you fired a long time ago for your conduct, Tim. You're fired."

"Wait— "

"Don't try to talk back, it'll only make things worse."

Tim nods, a look of defeat in his eyes. "Understood, Mr. Wright, Miss Medina," he mutters.

"Oh, and Josh?" Carter says with a grin, "I hear that your newest hotels aren't doing so well. Have you considered selling to a competitor? I think I could turn them into something beautiful."

Josh scowls but says nothing.

Josh and Tim's reactions confirm that we have the upper hand. For the first time in a long while, I feel confident and in control. The threat they posed is eliminated. We've managed to turn their attempts to intimidate us back on themselves.

As we exit the meeting room, relief washes over me. Melissa, Carter, and I pause outside the door, taking a moment to process what just happened.

"Was that enough, do you think?" I ask, seeking validation for our actions.

Melissa nods, a satisfied smile on her face. "Definitely. You were strong and clear. They'd be foolish to try anything now."

Carter wraps an arm around my shoulder, giving it a reassuring squeeze. "You handled that brilliantly, Megan. I don't think we'll be hearing from either of them any time soon."

Their support and confidence buoy me, solidifying my sense of accomplishment. We have faced our adversaries and come out on top. The sense of unity and strength we share as a team, as a family, is more evident than ever.

"We should celebrate," Melissa suggests, her eyes bright. "A victory like this deserves recognition."

I smile, feeling lighter, freer. "I couldn't agree more. Dinner, on me."

As we walk out of the hotel, optimism fills me. The challenges we faced only served to strengthen our bonds and our resolve. With Carter and Melissa by my side, I'm ready to take on whatever the future holds. Our journey together, marked by trials and triumphs, is just beginning, and I look forward to every step we will take, together.

Later that evening, at a bustling steakhouse, Melissa, Carter, and I find ourselves in a cozy booth, a celebratory air enveloping us. The clink of glasses and the sizzle of steaks from the open kitchen add to the lively atmosphere. We order drinks—a round of fine red wine—and peruse the menu, the tension from earlier completely dissipated.

As we wait for our meal, a genuine sense of camaraderie fills our conversation. We share stories and jokes, the laughter coming easily and naturally. It's a moment of normalcy, a cherished break from the recent chaos.

"I have to admit," I say, swirling the wine in my glass, "I wasn't sure how today was going to turn out. I'm glad it's all behind us now."

Carter reaches across the table, his hand finding mine. "You were incredible today, Megan. You stood up to them with such strength and grace. I couldn't be prouder."

His words warm my heart, and I squeeze his hand in response. "Thank you, Carter. I couldn't have done it without you and Melissa."

Melissa, who had been quietly observing our interaction, smiles at us. "You two are really cute together, you know that? Maybe I was wrong about you, Carter."

A blush creeps up my cheeks, but I can't hide the smile that forms on my lips. Carter's gaze meets mine, filled with affection and a hint of amusement.

"Well, I think we make a pretty great team," he says, his eyes twinkling.

The waiter arrives with our steaks drawing our attention momentarily. As we dig into our meal, the conversation flows effortlessly. We discuss future plans, lighter topics, and shared interests. The laughter and joy that surrounds the table are infectious, creating a bubble of happiness around us.

The evening progresses, and as we enjoy our dessert—a decadent chocolate lava cake—I realize how much my life has changed since meeting Carter. The challenges we've faced together have brought us closer, forging a bond that feels both exciting and comforting.

Outside the steakhouse, the evening air is crisp and unusually chilly, a stark contrast to the warmth we've just left behind. I instinctively wrap my arms around myself, shivering slightly. Carter notices immediately and, without hesitation, removes his coat and drapes it over my shoulders. The coat is warm and comforting, carrying his scent.

"Thank you," I say, looking up at him. In a spontaneous moment of gratitude, I rise onto my tiptoes and plant a soft kiss on his cheek. His smile in response is gentle and filled with warmth.

Melissa, who has been watching us with a fond smile, hails a taxi that pulls up to the curb. "I'll see you both soon," she says, opening the door. "I'm just a phone call away if you need anything."

Before stepping into the taxi, she pauses and looks back at us. "You know, I wasn't sure about you two at first. Seeing you together now, it's clear how much you mean to each other. I'm really happy for you both."

Her words bring a swell of happiness to my heart. "Thanks, Melissa. That means a lot to both of us," I reply, feeling Carter's hand gently squeeze my waist in agreement.

With a final wave, Melissa closes the taxi door, and the vehicle pulls away, leaving Carter and I alone on the sidewalk.

The street is quiet, the hustle of the city seeming distant. Carter turns to me, his eyes soft in the dim light of the streetlamps. "This feels like the start of something new, doesn't it?" he muses.

I nod, leaning into him. "It does. I feel like everything before this was just leading up to where we are right now."

He wraps his arms around me, pulling me close. "I never thought I'd find someone who could turn my world upside down in the best possible way. You've changed my whole life, Megan."

I rest my head against his chest, listening to the steady rhythm of his heart. "You've shown me that taking a chance on the unexpected can lead to something wonderful."

We stand there for a moment, embracing in the quiet of the night. As we finally pull apart, Carter holds my gaze. "Come on, let's get you home. It's been a long day."

The car ride back to my apartment is filled with a comfortable silence, the kind that comes from a deep sense of understanding and connection. As the city lights pass by outside, I find myself lost in thought, reflecting on how much has changed since Carter came into my life.

Walking into the building, the warmth of the lobby is a welcome contrast to the chill outside. As we step into the elevator and ascend to my floor, there's a noticeable feeling of anticipation between us.

Exiting the elevator, we make our way down the hallway to my apartment. Once inside, Carter closes the door behind us and turns to face me. At that moment, there's a shift in the air and the charged energy that's been building throughout the evening is ready to be released.

Carter steps closer, his hands finding my waist as he draws me toward him. Our lips meet in a kiss that's different from any we've shared before. It's deep and urgent, a physical expression of the emotions we've been holding back. He deftly unbuttons my blouse, his fingers gentle yet confident. The fabric falls open, and the kiss deepens, fueled by a shared desire that's been simmering beneath the surface for far too long.

I lead him to the bedroom, our movements synchronized. Once inside, Carter lifts me effortlessly, a playful smirk on his lips. He gently drops me onto the bed, and I laugh, the sound light and carefree.

"Someone's eager," I tease, looking up at him with a mixture of affection and desire.

He grins, climbing onto the bed beside me. "Only for you, Megan. I've been thinking about this all through dinner."

As Carter leans over me, his eyes lock with mine, filled with love and a hint of wonder. "This has been a wild ride, but it's more than worth it for you," he whispers, his voice laced with desire.

I reach up, tracing the line of his jaw with my fingers. "Wild is an understatement," I reply, my heart fluttering.

As Carter continues to explore my body with a gentle yet assertive touch, a wave of arousal floods over me. His fingers trace patterns on my skin, igniting a fire within me that grows with every stroke. I find myself lost in the intensity of the moment, every touch sending a thrill through me.

"Ready?" he asks, and I can barely manage a muffled *yes*.

The sensation of him entering me has a gasp spilling from my lips, back arching as he begins to thrust. His hands curl around my wrists, pinning me to the bed as I desperately try to match his pace.

"Carter," I whisper between kisses, hips arching into his, "you have no idea what you do to me."

He smiles against my lips, his breath warm on my skin. "Megan, the feeling is mutual."

As he leans down to kiss me again, I feel a sense of surrender, a willingness to let go and immerse myself fully in the moment. His kisses trail down my neck, eliciting a soft sigh from me. "You make me feel so cherished," I murmur, running my hands over the muscles of his back.

"You make me feel alive in ways I never knew possible," he replies, his voice heavy with emotion.

His thrusts are erratic now, the desperation obvious in the way his back arches, his lean body shining with sweat. He's never looked more appealing.

We come together; my head thrown back as Carter empties himself inside of me. As we lie intertwined, basking in the afterglow of our connection, Carter wraps his arms around me, pulling me close against his chest. I rest my head on his shoulder, feeling a sense of contentment and security.

In the quiet of the room, with only the soft sounds of our breathing and the distant hum of the city outside, I feel a profound sense of peace. Lying there with Carter, I'm filled with a deep appreciation for the unexpected twists and turns in life that have led me to this moment.

"We've come a long way, haven't we?" I say softly, tracing idle patterns on his chest.

"We have," he agrees, his voice tinged with wonder. "And I wouldn't change a thing."

As we drift off to sleep, held in each other's embrace, I feel a deep sense of gratitude and love. This journey with Carter, unpredictable and surprising, has been the most beautiful adventure of my life. And as I close my eyes, I dream about all the tomorrows we'll share together.

Chapter Twenty-Three

Carter

I wake up to the soft light filtering through the curtains and the comforting warmth of Megan sleeping beside me. As I reach for my phone, I notice a text from my brother. I contemplate responding but decide it can wait. Right now, the peaceful moment with Megan is all that matters.

Gently, I lean over and kiss her, stirring her awake. Her eyes flutter open, meeting mine with a sleepy smile. "Good morning," I whisper.

"Morning," she replies, her voice soft. She stretches languidly, the sheets falling away to reveal the contours of her body, still flush with the memories of last night.

"Do you want breakfast?" I ask, my gaze lingering on her.

She nods, a playful glimmer in her eyes. "Only if it's made by you."

I grin and lean in for another kiss, this one deeper, more lingering.

Reluctantly pulling away, I head into her little kitchen. As I start to prepare breakfast, my phone rings. Seeing my father's number on the screen, a knot forms in my stomach. I hesitate for a moment before answering.

"Carter," my father's voice comes through, more forceful than I expected. "I need to see you. Come to the hospital."

I rub the back of my neck, feeling the weight of his demand. "I'll be there soon, Dad," I reply, though every part of me wants to do the opposite.

After ending the call, I head back upstairs to tell Megan. She's sitting up in bed, the sheets pooled around her waist, looking every bit as beautiful as the night before.

"My father wants to see me," I say, a hint of reluctance in my voice. "I need to go to the hospital."

Megan's expression softens with understanding. "I'll come with you," she offers, her hand reaching out to mine.

I take her hand, grateful for her support. "Are you sure? It might not be pleasant."

She nods firmly. "I'm sure. We're in this together, remember?"

Her words bring a sense of comfort, a reminder of the strength we've found in each other. As we get ready to face the day, and to face whatever my father might throw our way, I feel a sense of resolve. With Megan by my side, I can handle anything.

Together, Megan and I make our way to the hospital, the morning air crisp and clear, a stark contrast to the turmoil of emotions churning inside me. As we walk in from the parking lot, Megan's presence by my side is a comforting constant, her strength bolstering my own.

We arrive at the hospital and find my father in his room, looking notably better than the last time I saw him. He's sitting up in bed, a variety of tubes and monitors are still attached to him, but there's a certain clarity in his eyes that wasn't there before.

"Dad, you're looking better," I remark cautiously as we approach.

He manages a weak smile. "Yes, I'm out of the woods, they say. The antibiotics are heavy, but they are doing their job."

I nod, relieved to hear he's recovering, though the atmosphere in the room remains tense. Megan stands beside me, her hand finding mine and giving it a reassuring squeeze.

After a brief pause, I get to the point. "You wanted to see me. What's going on?"

Dad's eyes dart to the framed photos on the bedside table. Pictures of Colton, his wife, and their two kids. A perfect little family. "He has a family, Carter. A wife, children. And he needs the money. You don't." I feel Megan's grip tighten slightly, a silent support as we both wait for what comes next.

"However," my father continues, "if you were to marry Megan now, as we agreed, the inheritance would go to you. I made a deal, and I won't go back on my word."

I take a moment to process his words, feeling a surge of frustration. "Dad, I'm not going to rush my relationship with Megan just for your inheritance. Not anymore. All you're doing is trying to pit Colton and I against each other."

My father looks surprised, perhaps he had been expecting me to jump at the opportunity. "You're serious about this, aren't you? About her?"

I nod, my resolve firm. "Yes, I am. What Megan and I have; it's real. I won't jeopardize that for money or for your approval. I love her, and that's what matters most to me now."

The room falls into a thoughtful silence. Megan gives my hand another squeeze, a gesture of solidarity that fills me with warmth.

My father finally speaks, his voice softer than before. "I see. I suppose I had you pegged all wrong, Carter. Perhaps there are things more important than money and legacy."

Megan, standing firmly beside me, speaks up with a respectful yet firm tone. "Mr. Wright, Carter has changed. He's grown beyond the need to be in anyone's shadow, even yours."

My father's eyes flicker between us, a hint of surprise in his expression. "I've always known you to be focused on success, on money, Carter. This is a side of you I never expected to see."

The comment stirs something in me, a mix of irritation and a need to assert my newfound perspective. "Maybe that's because you never really took the time to see me, Dad. You had your expectations, and I tried to meet them. That's not who I am, not anymore."

Finally, after a tense back-and-forth, my father sighs, a look of resignation crossing his face. "Perhaps I've been wrong about a few things," he admits, his voice softer. "If you've found happiness, Carter, in a way that's true to you, then I'm... I'm happy for you."

The admission is so unexpected, so out of character for the man I've known all my life, that it leaves me momentarily speechless. Megan squeezes my hand, her presence a grounding force.

"Thank you, Dad," I manage to say, the words feeling strange yet right.

As Megan and I leave the hospital room, I feel a mix of emotions. My father's grudging acceptance, while not a complete validation, is a step in a direction I never anticipated. It's a crack in the walls of our strained relationship, a glimmer of understanding that I hadn't dared hope for.

Walking beside Megan, I feel a sense of uncertainty about where our relationship stands in the grand scheme of things, but also a prevailing belief that we're on the right track. "That went better than I expected," I say to Megan, trying to make sense of it all.

"It did," she agrees, her tone reflective. "It seems like you're both starting to understand each other a little better."

I nod, taking in her words. "Maybe. It's going to take time to fully come to terms with all of this."

Walking hand in hand away from the hospital, the cool air of the outside world feels refreshing after the emotionally charged atmosphere in my father's room. Megan's presence beside me is a source of comfort and strength.

"I'm really proud of you, Carter," Megan says, her voice sincere. "Facing your father like that, standing up for what you believe in... it's a big step. Maybe this is the beginning of repairing your relationship with him. Who knows, maybe even Colton will come around someday."

I chuckle at the thought, a mix of skepticism and hope in my voice. "Let's not get our hopes too high about Colton just yet. One family reconciliation at a time."

Megan laughs, her mood light and relaxed. "Fair enough; but you never know, life is full of surprises. You know," Megan observes, "I've noticed a change in you since you talked to your dad. You seem... lighter, somehow."

I ponder her words for a moment, realizing she's right. "I guess I feel like I've finally started to break away from the expectations that have always been a burden. It's freeing, in a way I didn't expect."

She smiles, giving my hand a gentle squeeze. "That's what happens when you start living for yourself and not for someone else's approval. You find a new kind of freedom."

Her insight strikes a chord in me, echoing the thoughts and feelings I've been grappling with. "You've been a big part of that change, Megan. You've helped me see things in a new light, to understand what's truly important."

My change and growth are real and tangible, not just in my relationship with my father, but in every aspect of my life. Megan has been the catalyst for much of my transformation, her influence guiding me toward a more authentic version of myself.

As we reach her apartment, I realize that our journey together is just beginning. There's so much more to explore, to learn about each other, and to experience together. As I look at Megan, her eyes bright with optimism and affection, I feel a profound sense of gratitude and excitement for all the days to come. With her by my side, the future holds endless possibilities.

Chapter Twenty-Four

Megan

Two months later, I'm sitting on the sofa beside Carter in my apartment, a sense of contentment enveloping us. In my hands, I hold a bundle of photographs from the Davis-Barker wedding. As we flip through the photos together, a warm sense of pride fills me, seeing how the couple's happiness radiates in every image.

"Look at this one," I say, pointing to a photo where the couple is laughing, lost in their own world. "They look so genuinely happy. It's moments like these that remind me why I love my work."

Carter leans in, his arm draped casually around my shoulder. "You did an amazing job with their wedding, Megan, in such a short time. It's no wonder they look so happy. And I've hardly seen you!"

I smile, leaning into him. "Thank you. It was a lot of work, but seeing the end result makes it all worthwhile."

As we continue to look through the photos, I wonder at how much has changed. The challenges with Tim and Josh, my evolving relationship with Carter, it all seems like a whirlwind that has brought me to this peaceful moment.

Carter picks up a photo of the couple during their first dance and chuckles. "We should take notes for our own wedding. What do you think?"

I playfully nudge him, a laugh escaping my lips. "Let's not get ahead of ourselves. We've just started dating for real."

Even as I say it, my eyes drift down to my bare hand. It feels strange not to be wearing the engagement ring he got me—but when the time comes, I'm sure Carter will pull out all the stops for our *real* engagement.

He grins, his eyes twinkling with mischief. "I know, I know; but you have to admit, the idea isn't that far-fetched."

I look at him, the love I feel for him clear and unwavering. "Not far-fetched at all. I do know I love you, and the thought of marrying you someday doesn't scare me. It actually feels... right. Let's enjoy the journey we're on now, without rushing things though."

Carter nods, his expression tender. "I couldn't agree more. I love you, Megan, and wherever this journey takes us, I'm just happy to be on it with you." He pauses momentarily, clearly mulling something over in his head. "Just out of curiosity, if I were to buy a ring, you know, for the future, would you mind?"

I look into his eyes, seeing the earnestness and love reflected in them. A smile spreads across my face, a mix of happiness and anticipation at the thought. "I wouldn't mind at all, Carter. In fact, I'd love that. I plan on being with you for the long haul."

His face lights up at my response, and he leans in closer. "That's all I needed to hear," he says softly.

Carter's lips find mine in a tender kiss that quickly ignites into something more passionate. The initial innocence of the kiss gives way to a burning intensity as we lose ourselves in each other. My hands find their way into his hair, pulling him closer, and deepening our connection.

The world around us fades as we kiss, the warmth of our embrace enveloping us. It's a moment of pure connection, a physical manifestation of the love and commitment we've just expressed.

As we finally pull apart, breathless and flushed, I rest my forehead against his. "I love you, Carter," I whisper.

He smiles, his eyes shining with the same love and excitement. "I love you too, Megan."

In that moment, with the promise of a shared future hanging in the air, I feel a sense of peace wash over me. Our journey has been unexpected and full of surprises, but it has brought us to this beautiful place in our lives.

As we sit here, wrapped in each other's arms, the possibilities of our future together play out in my mind. A future filled with love, laughter, and the joy of being with the one person who understands and completes me in every way.

I grin up at him, before diving in for another kiss. It sends a thrill through me, desire pooling low in my stomach, and much lower.

As our kiss deepens, the intensity between us grows, a deep passion that seems to ignite with every touch. I kiss Carter again, pouring all my emotions into the embrace. His response is immediate, his hands roaming over my back, pulling me closer.

In a fluid movement, Carter shifts, flipping us over so that he is on top, his body pressing gently against mine as we lay entwined on the sofa. The change in position only heightens my arousal and I arch into him.

His lips trail from my mouth down my neck, each kiss sending waves of desire coursing through me. I tilt my head back, giving him more access, lost in the sensations he's eliciting. His hands tangle in my hair, a gentle yet assertive touch that sends shivers down my spine.

Feeling bold and wanting to mark him as mine, I lean up and press my lips against his neck. My teeth graze his skin lightly before I suck in a patch of skin, leaving a hickey. It's a small act of possession, one that speaks of the deep desire and love I feel for him.

Carter lets out a soft groan, the sound vibrating against my skin. His hand moves to cup my face, his thumb stroking my cheek tenderly. The contrast between the fervor of our actions and the tenderness in his touch is breathtaking.

Our breathing becomes ragged, the air around us charged with an intense desire that's both exhilarating and overwhelming. Every touch, every kiss, is imbued with a love that's been growing for weeks now.

"Megan," Carter breathes out, his voice thick with emotion. "You have no idea how much you mean to me."

I reach up, tracing the line of his jaw with my fingertips. "Show me," I whisper, a challenge and an invitation all at once.

He answers with another kiss, this one even more passionate than the last. Our bodies move together in a rhythm that feels as natural as breathing, our hips grinding together.

Carter becomes even more excited, his movements reflecting a deep, desperate need. I am completely lost in the torrent of emotions and sensations, swept away by the passion that Carter ignites in me.

The world around us dissolves, leaving only the two of us in our own private universe, bound together by an overwhelming connection. I respond to Carter, my own actions mirroring his urgency. The sensations are intense, almost overwhelming, but I surrender to them, to him, completely.

Eventually, we break apart, both of us breathing heavily, our cheeks flushed with the heat of our passion. Carter leans in and tenderly kisses my forehead, a gentle contrast to the intensity of moments ago. I smile at him, feeling a profound sense of connection and affection.

We lay in a comfortable silence for a while, simply enjoying each other's presence. The emotional and physical intensity of our encounter leaves us both in a state of contented quietude.

After a time, Carter rolls off me, propping himself up on one elbow as he looks down at me. "I understand why you want to take things slow, especially considering what happened with your ex," he says softly. "I want you to know, I'm really excited to see where things go with us."

His words fill me with a sense of warmth and reassurance. I reach out, tracing the outline of his face with my fingers. "I'm excited too, Carter. What we have is special, and I don't want to rush it. I want to relish every moment, every step we take together."

He smiles, his eyes reflecting the same emotions I feel. "Relishing every moment with you sounds perfect to me."

As we lie here, talking about our future, our hopes, and our dreams, I feel a sense of optimism and joy. With Carter, I've found not just a partner but a true companion, someone who understands and complements me in every way.

After lounging together for a while, basking in the afterglow of our intense connection, Carter sits up with an excited glint in his eyes. "So, what do you think about dinner? I want to take you out on a proper date. You've been so busy with the wedding, this is our first chance for a proper dinner date as a real couple."

The idea instantly brings a smile to my face. "I'd love that. Where did you have in mind?"

He thinks for a moment, then his face lights up with an idea. "How about *Estrella*? I've heard their rooftop dining experience is unparalleled, and the view of the city is supposed to be breathtaking."

I raise my eyebrows in surprise. *Estrella* is one of the city's most exclusive and expensive restaurants, known for its exquisite cuisine and stunning views. "Carter, that place is incredibly fancy..."

He nods enthusiastically. "Absolutely. I want to show you off, spoil you. You deserve the best, Megan. Also, I've never been there so it would be a first-time experience for both of us that we can share together."

Despite my initial hesitation, the earnestness in his voice and the excitement in his eyes are too much to resist. I laugh, the idea of such an extravagant date both thrilling and a little overwhelming. "Okay, okay, you've convinced me. Only if you promise not to make a habit of such extravagance. I don't need fancy restaurants to enjoy our time together."

Carter leans in, giving me a quick kiss. "I promise. Tonight, I want to give you an experience you'll never forget."

With that settled, the anticipation for our date adds a new layer of excitement to the day. We both get up, starting to get ready for the evening. I find myself caught up in the thrill of it all—getting dressed up, going out to a place I've only dreamed of visiting, and most importantly, being there with Carter.

As I stand in front of the mirror, choosing my outfit for the evening, Carter comes up behind me, wrapping his arms around my waist. He looks at our reflection, a satisfied smile on his face. "You're going to be the most beautiful woman there," he says, his voice filled with pride and affection.

I lean back into him, feeling his warmth. "You'll be the most handsome guy," I reply, meeting his gaze in the mirror.

Our reflection, side by side, feels like a symbol of our relationship—two individuals, each with their own strengths and vulnerabilities, coming together to create something beautiful and strong.

Once we are both ready, I take a moment to stand in front of the mirror with Carter, admiring how we look together. My hair falls loosely around my shoulders, complementing the elegant simplicity of my black dress. Beside me, Carter stands dashing in a black suit, paired with a crisp white shirt, his hair charmingly tousled.

I can't help but smile at our reflections. "We clean up pretty well, don't we?" I remark, a playful note in my voice.

Carter looks at me through the mirror, his eyes twinkling with amusement. "I'd say more than just *pretty well*. You look stunning, Megan. I'm just trying to keep up."

I laugh, turning to face him. "Well, I think you're doing more than just keeping up. You look incredibly handsome."

He steps closer, his hands finding my waist. "Only the best for tonight," he says, his gaze softening. "After all, I'm with the most beautiful woman in the city."

I feel a blush creep up my cheeks at his words. It's still surreal, how genuine and deep our relationship has become, how naturally these moments of affection and compliments come to us now.

"We should get going, or we'll miss our reservation," I say, though a part of me wants to stay wrapped in this moment forever.

Carter nods, releasing me reluctantly. "You're right. Let's not keep *Estrella* waiting."

Epilogue

Megan

Two Years Later

The last two years have flown by, and as I sit in my well-appointed office, meeting with two new clients, I reflect on how much my business has grown. The couple sitting across from me, Skye and Benjamin, are looking to plan their dream wedding, and their excitement is obvious.

"So, we were thinking of a spring wedding, outdoors, maybe in a botanical garden?" Skye suggests, her eyes sparkling at the idea.

"That sounds absolutely beautiful," I respond enthusiastically. "Spring weddings have such a lovely atmosphere, and a botanical garden will provide the perfect backdrop. The natural beauty will enhance the romance and elegance of your day."

Benjamin nods, his hand intertwined with Skye's. "We also want to make sure it's a fun day for our guests, not too formal. Kind of a celebration of love and life, you know?"

I smile at their vision. "Absolutely, I understand. We can certainly weave in elements that will make it a joyous and memorable event for everyone. How about interactive stations or lawn games during the cocktail hour? It'll add a playful touch to the elegance."

Their faces light up at the suggestion. "That sounds amazing!" Skye exclaims. "You clearly know what you're doing. We're so glad we chose you to be our planner."

As we continue discussing ideas, Skye's gaze drifts to my hand, noticing the ring on my finger. It's a massive platinum and diamond wedding ring, a testament to the love and life I've built with Carter.

"That's a gorgeous ring," she comments. "Is it new?"

I glance down at it, a warm rush of happiness filling me. "Thank you, and no, it's not new. Carter and I got married last year. It was a summer wedding."

Her eyes widen in delight. "You're married! That's wonderful. I bet it was a beautiful wedding."

"It really was," I say, a blush coloring my cheeks. "It was everything we wanted! Planning my own wedding was quite the experience, given my profession."

Benjamin chuckles. "I can imagine. Must have been like a chef cooking their own meal."

I laugh along with them. "Exactly! It gave me even more insight into what my clients go through. It was a beautiful journey."

I think back to the wedding; it was a beautiful early summer wedding under a canopy of blossoming trees, at one of the Vivante's newest hotels. I had looked beautiful in my flowing wedding dress—and Carter had been absolutely enchanting in a gorgeous fitted suit, hair swept back. Everyone had been there, and although his father is still on a long road to recovery after his health scare, he and Colton sat with the family in the front row.

It really couldn't have been more perfect.

The conversation flows effortlessly as we delve deeper into planning their wedding. My own experiences, both professional and personal, help guide the ideas and suggestions I offer. As the meeting comes to an end, Skye and Benjamin look thrilled with the plans we've begun to sketch out.

"We're so excited to start this journey with you, Megan. Thank you for everything today," Skye says as they stand to leave.

"It's my pleasure," I reply, standing up to see them out. "I'm just as excited to bring your dream wedding to life."

As they leave, I sit back down, feeling a deep sense of fulfillment.

Then my phone buzzes with an incoming call from Carter. Smiling, I answer, already feeling a rush of happiness at the sound of his voice.

"Hey, love. I was thinking of coming over with lunch. What are you in the mood for? Italian or Mexican?" Carter asks, his tone playful.

I consider for a moment, my current cravings weighing heavily on my decision. "Hmm, how about Italian? Some pasta sounds amazing right now."

"Your wish is my command," he replies cheerfully. "I'll pick up the best pasta in town. Extra Parmesan for you?"

I laugh. "You know me too well. See you soon."

As I end the call, I'm grateful for Carter's constant support and care, especially now. I glance down at my slightly swollen belly, a gentle reminder of the new life we're going to welcome into our world.

Before long, I hear a knock on my office door. It's my next client, Brandon Wallace, arriving for his appointment. I stand up to greet him, and we share an awkward but warm embrace, my baby bump creating a slight barrier.

"I swear, your bump keeps growing. When are you due again?" Brandon asks, smiling as he steps back.

"September," I reply, my hand instinctively resting on my belly.

"That's wonderful news," he says, his eyes bright with genuine happiness.

We sit down to discuss the details of his upcoming wedding. As we talk, I feel a flutter of movement from the baby, a sensation that never fails to bring a smile to my face.

The conversation is interrupted by another knock on the door, and Carter enters, carrying a bag filled with the aroma of Italian food. "Lunch is served," he announces, grinning.

"Brandon, this is my husband, Carter," I introduce them.

"Pleasure to meet you," Carter says, extending his hand for a handshake.

"Likewise, it's not often I get to meet a guy like Carter Wright of the Vivante hotels."

Carter laughs. "Yes, well, I've taken a bit of a backseat as of late. My brother and I are co-owners now, but in truth he handles most of the difficult stuff now. Turns out he's a natural."

"Oh, early retirement?"

"Not as such. I'm thinking of it as a sabbatical of sorts."

"Well, congrats on that—and congratulations on the baby too," Brandon responds.

Carter sets the food down on my desk and then turns to me, his hand gently caressing my belly. "How's our little one doing?"

"Active as ever," I reply, covering his hand with mine.

Brandon watches us with a smile. "You two seem like a great team."

"We try our best," Carter says, looking at me with affection.

I smile up at him, feeling an overwhelming sense of love and contentment. "We do make a pretty good team, don't we?"

As Brandon leaves and Carter and I sit down to enjoy our lunch, I'm excited for all the future holds—for our expanding family, for my business, and for the endless possibilities that life with Carter offers. Each day is a new adventure, and I'm grateful for every moment we spend together.

We sit and enjoy our Italian lunch, the playful banter between Carter and I flows effortlessly. "You're going to be such a great dad," I say, watching him with a smile.

He grins, his eyes sparkling. "I'll do my best."

Our laughter fills the room, creating a warm, joyful atmosphere. Amidst our conversation, I remember to ask about his plans for later in the day.

"Are you visiting your father later?" I inquire, knowing the relationship between them is still a work in progress.

Carter nods, his expression turning a bit more serious. "Yeah, I am. Things have been rocky, but I think they're slowly getting better. We're talking more, at least. Colton and I still don't really talk about anything but business, but I'm starting to feel like things are on the mend with Dad."

"That's good to hear," I respond, reaching across the table to squeeze his hand. "Do you want me to come with you?"

He appreciates the offer, his smile warm. "Thanks, but... this is something I need to do alone. It's part of the process, you know?"

I nod, understanding completely. "Of course."

After we finish our lunch, Carter insists on helping me tidy up. He clears the table and takes care of the trash, his movements thoughtful and caring. I watch him for a moment, feeling a surge of love and gratitude for this man who has become my partner in every sense of the word.

After he finishes cleaning up, I stand beside him, resting my head against his shoulder. "Thank you for lunch, and for everything," I say softly.

He wraps an arm around me, pulling me close. "It's my pleasure, Megan. I just want to take care of you and our little one."

We stand there for a moment, wrapped in each other's arms, the quiet of the afternoon enveloping us. The journey we've been on together, from our unconventional beginning to where we are now, feels like a beautiful, winding path that's led us to this moment of peace and contentment.

After tidying up, Carter and I share a deep, affectionate kiss. As I pull away and head toward my desk to get back to work, he playfully slaps my ass, a mischievous glint in his eyes.

"Hey!" I protest with mock indignation, turning to give him a playful scowl.

"What? I can't help it. You're irresistible," he says with a grin, his eyes dancing with humor.

I laugh, shaking my head at his antics. "You're irresistible... and ridiculous, you know that?"

He shrugs, still grinning. "Ridiculously in love with you."

"Okay, Mr. Ridiculous, I should get back to work. What are your plans for the rest of the day?" I ask, sitting down at my desk.

Carter leans against the edge of the desk, his expression turning thoughtful. "Well, after visiting Dad, I was thinking I could pick you up from work. Maybe we could go do something fun together. Just the two of us."

"That sounds perfect," I reply, already looking forward to spending more time with him. "I'd love that."

"Great! It's a date then," he says, his smile infectious.

As he prepares to leave, we embrace once more. In the middle of our hug, a sudden movement from my belly makes us both pause. The baby kicks, a small but noticeable movement against my stomach.

Carter laughs, his hand moving to gently touch my belly. "Seems like someone wants to say hello."

I place my hand over his, feeling the warmth of his touch. "Or maybe they're just excited about our date too."

He kisses my forehead tenderly. "I'll see you later, love. Take care of yourself and our little kicker here."

"I will. Bye, Carter. Love you," I say, my heart full of warmth.

"Love you too," he replies before finally heading out the door.

As I watch him leave, a sense of peace and happiness envelops me. I'm struck by the beauty of our life together—the love we share, the family we're building, and the simple joys of everyday moments. I turn back to my work, but with a lightness in my heart, eagerly anticipating our evening together.

Later that day, as I'm packing up my things in the office, I hear a familiar knock on the door. Turning around, I see Carter standing there, his smile bright and full of warmth. Without a word, he strides over, sweeps me into his arms, and twirls me around. A delighted laugh escapes me, the spontaneity of his action catching me off guard.

"Carter! You're going to make me dizzy," I exclaim, still laughing as he sets me down gently.

"I just can't help it," he says, his eyes sparkling with joy. "I'm always so excited to see you."

I playfully roll my eyes, but my heart swells with affection. "Even with the extra baby weight?" I ask, half-teasing, half-serious.

He looks at me, his gaze soft and full of love. "Megan, you're as beautiful as ever. More so, even. There's something about you carrying our child that just takes my breath away."

His words wash over me, filling me with a sense of love and appreciation that goes beyond physical appearances. I reach up, pulling him into a deep, heartfelt kiss.

As we break away, he gently places his hand on my belly, feeling the gentle movements of our baby. "Are you ready for your scan tomorrow?"

Excitement swells inside of me. "Yes, we'll finally get to know the little one's gender."

"I think it might be more fun to let it be a surprise."

I laugh, reaching up to press a kiss to Carter's cheek. "Maybe it would be."

We stand there for a moment, lost in our little world, a world that has grown and evolved so beautifully in such a short time. From the first awkward and uncertain steps of our relationship to this moment of shared joy and anticipation for our growing family, every moment with Carter has been a journey of love, growth, and happiness.

"Well, are you ready for our date?" Carter asks, breaking the comfortable silence.

I nod, a wide smile spreading across my face. "Absolutely. Let's go."

Hand in hand, we leave my office, stepping into the evening together. As we walk, I reflect on the incredible journey we've shared. From a business arrangement to a deep, loving partnership, our story has been one of unexpected twists and beautiful turns.

With Carter, I'm now ready for whatever the future holds. Our love is a guiding light, leading us through challenges and triumphs alike. And as we embark on this next chapter of our lives, welcoming a new member into our family, I know that our journey will only continue to grow richer and more fulfilling.

Our story, a tale of love, understanding, and partnership, is a testament to the unexpected paths a courageous life can take you on. And as we step into the future together, I'm excited for all the adventures yet to come.

THE END

If you loved *Irresistible Silver Fox Billionaire*, you will love ***Damaged Silver Fox Billionaire.***

Scan this QR code to visit the Amazon page for
Damaged Silver Fox Billionaire

GWYNNE HART

Read chapter one of **_Damaged Silver Fox Billionaire_** on the very next page!

Sneak Peek Damaged Silver Fox Billionaire

Damaged Silver Fox Billionaire

New job as assistant to a silver fox billionaire? Check.
Playing his fake fiancée? Check.
Resisting the temptation to rip off his clothes? ... *Fail.*

As Killian Reilly's new personal assistant and his son's part-time nanny, I'm supposed keep things professional.

But when he adds the role of "fiancée" to my job description, all bets are off.

He's gorgeous, powerful, and one of L.A.'s hottest players.

To secure a high-stakes deal, he must prove his playboy days are over.

A weekend away, and in character from dawn to dusk, we seal the deal.
Buzzed with success, we barely make it to our suite before the clothes fly off.
Unleashed, our genuine attraction is fiery.

What's reality? We're like magnets, drawn together and inseparable.

But my ex-fiancé discovers our pretense and plots to sabotage the deal.

I fear his mischief will destroy our shot at true love.

Chapter One

Emily

"You have no idea what you're throwing away, Emily!" My mother's shrill voice cuts through the tiny apartment, bouncing off the bare walls. The conversation, or rather, argument, has been going on for the better part of an hour, and I'm bone-tired of it.

"Mom, you don't understand..." I begin, but she's not interested in understanding.

"No, you don't understand!" she barks back. "Matt Radford is a catch. He has everything, and he could've given *you* everything!"

I run a hand through my hair, frustration simmering. "I don't want 'everything', Mom. I want to be happy."

"And money doesn't make you happy?" she scoffs.

I picture her sitting in the lavish living room of our family estate, her face twisted in disapproval. "No, not without love."

A dramatic sigh resounds from the other end of the phone. "I thought I raised a smarter girl."

The jab stings, but I swallow down the hurt. "Love isn't about money, Mom."

"But life is, Emily!" she retorts. "You're twenty-eight. You've thrown away a golden opportunity, and for what? To be alone? To struggle?"

"I'd rather struggle than be stuck in a loveless marriage," I clench my fist around the phone.

"You'll regret this, Emily. You'll see what real struggle is like."

"Are you threatening me?" I ask, taken aback by the menace in her tone. She'd always been prone to angry flashes and snapping as if everything wrong in the world was my fault.

"No, darling," she purrs, and the feigned sweetness in her voice sends a chill down my spine. "Just saying... You've thrown away a perfectly good marriage, and you can't expect me to pick up the pieces you've tossed away. So if money doesn't make you happy, you'll have none of ours."

"What does that even mean?"

"It means, Emily, that you're on your own. You want to be alone? Then *be* alone. Your father and I will no longer help you dig your way out of your messes. Don't come to us crying for help when you realize you can't make it on your own."

I barely have time to respond before the line goes dead. Stunned, I lower my phone from my ear and stare at it in shock. Cut off, just like that. My chest tightens at the realization, but I refuse to cry. I won't give her that satisfaction.

I look around the small apartment, my new kingdom. It's not much, but it's mine. It's a testament to the decision I made, the path I chose. Alone and financially cut off, sure, but free to be myself.

My phone rings again, shattering the silence. The screen reads "Thomas," my older brother and now my only ally.

"Emily," he greets, worry seeping through his voice. "How did it go?"

"Mom cut me off," I say flatly, too exhausted to mask the hurt in my voice.

There's a brief silence on the other end, filled only by Thomas's uneven breaths. "I was afraid it would come to this," he finally admits, and the fact he's not surprised only makes it hurt worse.

"You knew?" I ask, a touch of resentment seeping into my tone.

"I... suspected," he says, and I can imagine him rubbing the back of his neck, a nervous habit he's had forever. Though there are fifteen years between us, we have always been close. "You know how they are, Emily. Our parents... they've always valued status and money over everything else. Love doesn't fit into their equation."

I let out a sigh, slumping onto my couch. "That's an understatement. Remember how Matt and I met at that big dinner?"

He laughs, but it's a hollow sound. "Practically an arranged marriage. Who would have thought we'd still have those in the twenty-first century?"

"Only in the Logan family," I reply, my laughter matching his with bitterness.

A comfortable silence settles over the phone. It's a shared understanding, an unspoken agreement of our parents' eccentricities. I rest my head back, staring blankly at the ceiling. I've been strong until now and put on a brave face, but now in the safety of Thomas's company, I let myself feel the fear, the uncertainty.

"Emily..." Thomas starts after a moment, his voice careful, "You won't be alone in this, okay? You've got me."

I smile, though he can't see it. "Thanks, Tommy."

Another silence, then, "There might be a way out of this."

My heart skips a beat. "What do you mean?"

"I spoke to Killian... Killian Reilly. He's looking for a new personal assistant. With your skills, your experience... It's a long shot, but..."

Killian Reilly. The name sends a wave of childhood memories rushing through me. Thomas's brilliant childhood friend. A transient presence in our young lives. And now, a billionaire, one of the most successful businessmen in Los Angeles. I know Thomas is no longer joined at the hip to Killian, but they still chat frequently.

The thought of working for Killian is daunting. The man has always been intimidating as hell, but desperation makes the decision for me. I can't afford to be picky. Not when the ghost of eviction is looming over my head.

"I'll do it," I say, clenching my phone tighter.

"Emily, you don't have to—"

"No," I interrupt him, "I do have to. I'm not going to sit here and feel sorry for myself. I won't give Mom and Dad the satisfaction. I'll take the job."

Thomas stays silent for a moment before finally sighing, "Alright, Emily. I'll let Killian know."

The call ends with a promise from Thomas to set up a meeting with Killian as soon as possible. I drop my phone onto the coffee table, staring blankly at the fading daylight outside my window. The world I once knew is crumbling around me, but amidst the wreckage, I can see opportunity.

Two days later, I am outside an enormous building in downtown Los Angeles. The Reilly Enterprises logo is embossed in shiny gold letters against a backdrop of polished black granite. The building looms high into the sky, reflecting the morning sunlight and giving an illusion of endlessness. I take a deep breath, steeling myself before pushing through the revolving doors.

Inside, the high-end décor and the swift movement of immaculately dressed people do nothing to calm my fraying nerves. I approach the receptionist's desk, clutching my purse tightly.

"I have an interview with Mr. Killian Reilly," I say, my voice stronger than I feel.

The receptionist barely glances my way. "For the job? It's in his alternate office. Elevator to the 30th floor, then left."

Alternate office? She offers no further instructions, already focusing on her next task. I mutter a thank you and make my way to the elevators, my heels clicking loudly against the marble floors.

Riding up, my stomach churns with each passing floor. The ding of the elevator arriving on the thirtieth-floor sounds like a gong in my ears. With a deep breath, I step out, following the receptionist's instructions.

Killian's office is at the end of the hallway—an imposing dark wooden door with a brass nameplate. I find it strange there's no secretary outside his office, no gatekeeper to the dragon's den.

I knock on the door, the sound echoing in the eerily quiet corridor. From within, I can hear the faint rustling of papers, the deep baritone of Killian's voice humming a response. It's an unfamiliar yet oddly comforting sound.

A few minutes pass, and still, no one opens the door. I knock again, louder this time. "Mr. Reilly?" I call out. There's a muffled response, but I can't make out the words.

I'm left in the hallway, standing awkwardly outside his office, my nerves slowly being replaced with irritation.

What the hell is he doing in there? I'm right on time, aren't I?

Checking my watch confirms it. I'm right on the dot. He's the one who's late for his own meeting. So much for being a punctual businessman.

With a huff, I lean against the wall opposite his door, arms crossed over my chest. I guess I'll just have to wait. It's not like I have anywhere else to be. Not when my job, my livelihood, is dependent on the man on the other side of this door. The man who's too busy to even greet me.

Just as I'm contemplating knocking again, the door swings open. Killian Reilly appears in the doorway, looking mildly surprised as if he's forgotten he was supposed to be meeting someone.

He's taller than I remember, his blond hair shot through with silver. His deep-set, stormy-gray eyes regard me with curiosity. There's a hint of annoyance there, too, as if my mere presence has disturbed him.

But God, he's handsome.

His clean-shaven face is sharp, chiseled, with high cheekbones and a strong jaw. His navy suit hugs his broad shoulders perfectly, the fabric straining slightly against his muscular build.

I take a moment to compose myself, pushing back the wave of heat that washes through me. This is Killian, my older brother's best friend, the annoying teenager I used to know.

Except he's not a teenager anymore. He's a man—and he's hot.

"Can I help you?" he asks, his deep voice pulling me from my thoughts.

"I..." I blink, suddenly finding it hard to form words. "I'm here for the interview?"

A look of realization dawns on his face. "Ah, of course. Come in," he says, holding the door wider and motioning for me to enter.

I step past him into the office, taking in the rich dark wood, the floor-to-ceiling windows displaying a breathtaking view of the Los Angeles skyline. The room smells of leather and expensive cologne, an intoxicating mix that has my heart fluttering.

Killian closes the door behind us, moving around the room to sit at his large mahogany desk. I don't think he recognizes me yet.

"So," he says, his tone all business. "Tell me, why should I hire you?"

His question throws me off. Not because it's a surprise—he's right to ask it, after all—but because there's no hint of recognition in his gaze. No acknowledgment he's even met me before.

He has no memory of the summer afternoons we spent together at my parents' pool over the years, especially the summer after he retired from the army. Granted, I was only fifteen at the time. He was my first teenage crush.

I clear my throat, pulling my features into a professional smile. "Well, Mr. Reilly," I begin, deciding not to correct his lapse in memory just yet. Let's see how this plays out. "I have a diverse range of skills," I begin, keeping my voice steady. "I'm organized, adaptable, and I know how to prioritize. I've worked in a fast-paced, high-stress environment for years, and I believe I would be a valuable asset to your team."

Killian leans back in his chair, considering me with a thoughtful expression. There's something odd about it, though, like he's seeing me in a light he hadn't expected. It's his next words that confirm my suspicions.

"You've worked with children before?" he asks, a hint of surprise in his voice.

"Children?" I repeat, confused.

"Yes, obviously you need to be well-versed in handling more... *difficult* children for this position."

I open my mouth to correct him—I'm not here for a nanny position—but he's already moving on with a rush of words that leaves me reeling.

"I've been struggling to find a suitable caretaker for Keagan. The last one couldn't handle his... energy. If you're willing to take on the role, I can assure you the compensation will be fair. It will involve relocating to my residence and being available for early mornings, school runs, evenings..."

His voice fades into the background as confusion swirls in my mind. Nanny? He thinks I'm here to be a nanny? That's not what I signed up for. I'd prepared to argue my case for the PA position, not childcare.

Before I can protest, Killian is rising from his chair and extending his hand.

"Well," he says, the businesslike tone back in his voice. "Welcome aboard. Let's consider this a probationary period to see if you're a good fit for our family dynamic. I'm desperate enough to admit I don't have much choice."

It's hardly a standing ovation. Still, my hand automatically rises to shake his, not failing to feel the jolt of electricity from his touch, but my brain is still trying to play catch-up. I'm hired? As a nanny?

Did you enjoy this sneak peek?

Scan this QR code to visit the Amazon page for
Damaged Silver Fox Billionaire

Thank You

I'm grateful that you have read ***Irresistible Silver Fox Billionaire***.

Reviews allow others to learn about my books (and keep me writing) so I would appreciate it if you could drop me an honest review on Amazon.

The QR code below will take you to this book's Amazon page.

It only takes a few seconds, and this is easiest way you can support my continued writing efforts.

If you are a romance bookworm and would like to receive an advance reader copy (ARC) of my future books, do sign up to join my ARC team at **gwynne.vip/arc**

> ***"Reading one book is like eating
> one potato chip."***
> **— Diane Duane**

Made in United States
Orlando, FL
11 May 2025

61198433R00127